FALLEN

A NOVEL

FALLEN

A NOVEL

MATTHEW RALEY

Kregel
Publications

Fallen: A Novel

© 2008 by Matthew Raley

Published by Kregel Publications, a division of Kregel, Inc., P.O. Box 2607, Grand Rapids, MI 49501.

Scripture taken from the King James Version.

Library of Congress Cataloging-in-Publication Data
Raley, Matthew.
Fallen : a novel / by Matthew Raley.
 p. cm.
 I. Title.
PS3618.A453F35 2007
813'.6—dc22   2007040337

ISBN 978-0-8254-3575-1

Printed in the United States of America

08 09 10 11 12 / 5 4 3 2 1

For Bridget Raley

I

With the punishing glare of the late afternoon sun glinting through my office window, I tried to stay engaged in the conversation across the desktop. Erin Flynn, my head teller, was chewing out Melissa, our bombshell-in-residence, for failing to balance her till umpteen times in her first three months at the bank. There were a few hundred bucks we couldn't account for today because Melissa couldn't find which transaction she'd misrecorded.

Flynn swept her gleaming dark hair behind her shoulder with mounting annoyance. Melissa was nearly in tears.

I drummed my fingers on the edge of the desk and perused the scene outside my window.

My office has a nice view of McKinley Avenue, the main drag through town. There's a traffic signal at the corner that stacks the cars up a few feet from my desk. I can look right through the windshields and see all the embarrassing things people do while they're waiting for the light to change. My window is one-way glass, so I can stare at the drivers without them staring back.

At the moment, the street was clear and I could see half a block down to Basic Bean, the trendy neighborhood coffee place. Two trendy Bean employees were outside, smoking on their break. A silver Mercedes pulled up and a guy got out on the passenger side.

There's Pastor Dave . . . but that's not his car.

He approached the two employees and they smiled at him like the regular customer he was. After he passed, they kept flashing glances back and forth between him and the car. Then they looked at each other and grinned.

Dave went into the Bean and the Mercedes drove on toward me. When the light changed, it stopped cheek-to-jowl with my vantage point. The driver was a woman—thirtyish—about Dave's age.

Because she wasn't Dave's wife, Amy—who would probably never notice a Mercedes, much less drive one—I studied the woman's face. I wanted a reason why Dave might've been a passenger in those leather seats of hers. Had I seen her at church? No, I hadn't. Was she maybe a relative of Dave's—a sister or something? No. She had a Mediterranean look, maybe Italian or Greek, and Dave Schmidt was German on both sides. Besides, neither Dave nor Amy had any siblings.

I kept studying her—fingers tapping a beat on the wheel, eyes hidden behind stylish shades. Her hair was done in a finger-in-the-light-socket style. I could tell the shoulder pads on her suit jacket were too big. I could even categorize her makeup. There's the business way, the streetwalker's way, and my wife's way. This gal was all business: bright, assertive, fluorescent.

Realtor. Maybe Dave and Amy are looking for a new house. Doesn't seem likely, but it's possible.

About the time she drove off, I realized that Flynn and Melissa had been looking at me in silence for who knows how long.

Think fast. "Uh, look, Melissa, we're not trying to roast you on a spit. I think what Flynn and I want to know is, why do you have so much trouble with your till? Is there some way we can help?"

Melissa's lip was quivering and her eyes started to glisten. "I don't know! I don't know! I guess I'm just not cut out for this. Like, I always got As in math? But now I, like, look at all those numbers and I just, like, freeze up. It's like . . ." This went on, getting more baffling, and more annoying, with each *like*.

I hate mysterious failings in otherwise capable employees. Melissa was great with customers. She remembered their names. She sold a lot of services. She kept the line moving. And she didn't goof off. But for some reason she couldn't concentrate on balancing her till.

I have an absolute policy: never throw a person away. Dispel the mystery around the failing. Help the person succeed. Look for the win-win.

Melissa kept on until she said something I couldn't overlook. "You may as well just fire me—or let me quit."

"Okay, let's stop right there. We're not going to fire you, and we're definitely not going to let you quit. We're going to figure out why you're having trouble with your till and we're going to fix it."

Her eyes got wide under her tweezed brows. I doubt anyone had ever talked to her that way. Flynn gave me one of her bland smiles and looked away.

I leaned forward, modulating my voice. "I've noticed that you seem rushed when you balance your till. In fact, you race through it. Your shoulders hunch, you get flushed, your fingers get white around your pen. It's no wonder you can't find your mistakes. What's the hurry?"

"Well, my boyfriend picks me up at a quarter after five. I'm afraid he'll be upset if I keep him waiting."

"You're afraid?"

"He gets, like, totally—"

"You're afraid he's going to yell at you?"

"Yeah." Her melodic tone said, "Duh!"

"Melissa, what does he say when he yells at you? Does he yell at you a lot?"

"He's not, like, abusive? I mean, he doesn't, like, actually yell. He doesn't really *say* anything."

"So you're afraid he's going to yell, but he never does."

"He just drives really wild."

"Does that frighten you?"

"No. But it's like his veins totally flare. What is it with guys?"

"What do you mean?"

"Why can't they just chill? It's like everything's about *them.* Their needs. Their money. Their time. Like nobody else has problems."

I glanced at Flynn. Her eyes asked, *Yeah, what is it with guys?*

"Um, we men can be a little intense, I guess. You're sure he isn't abusive? He doesn't yell unkind things at you?"

"Not at *me.*"

"Oh? Who then?"

"He mostly yells at you."

"Ah." I didn't need to look at Flynn. Her jibes worked telepathically.

"I just don't want to set him off."

"So you rush through balancing the till so he won't have to wait?"

"Yeah."

"So instead of having him wait a few extra minutes while you carefully count out your till, he sits there for half an hour while you rebalance the thing ten times."

"Pretty much."

"Okay, how about this? You tell him that we had this little talk, and that I realized I was wasting his time. We decided he should pick you up at five-thirty, instead of a quarter after. Would that be better, or do you want it even later?"

"No, that's fine."

"This won't mess up his schedule even worse?"

"No."

"You'll slow down and concentrate?"

"Yeah."

"Alrighty then."

She grabbed a Kleenex from the box on the corner of my desk and walked out.

"Flynn, tell the girls no more cleavage."

She peered at me over the rims of her glasses. "Define cleavage."

———————

Through two more meetings, I couldn't get the problem of the woman in the Mercedes out of my mind. For a while I tried to convince myself that a pastor might sometimes ride in a Mercedes with a woman who's not his wife. I thought again about the possibility of a real estate transaction, but it didn't add up. As chairman of the church board of trustees, I was fairly certain I would have heard if the pastor and his wife were looking for a new home. And even if I hadn't heard, why wasn't Amy in the car with them? The more I tried to imagine other scenarios, the more implausible everything seemed. Car trouble? Lady stops to help? No. She'd never stop for a man. Stuck at a meeting without a ride? No. The kind of meetings Dave would attend would be mostly men—men from the church. Even if the gal in the Mercedes were at such a meeting, she'd never offer him a ride.

I've ridden with women in a group situation—going with the girls from the bank to a luncheon, for instance. It's the sort of thing people joke about but never seriously question.

But when I'm alone with a woman, I'm very aware of my personal space—and my eyes.

Like elevators. Say I'm rushing to get in before the doors close, and when I'm right on top of them I realize there's a woman all by herself in there. At that speed I can't stop or turn around without looking cartoonish. I have to go in. And the shorter the skirt, the higher I have to look. I have to watch the numbers change like they're the most fascinating things since TV. I don't even breathe. And an elevator is a far sight different from being alone with a woman in her Mercedes. I felt it was a problem, Dave's being in that car.

I admit I'm old-fashioned. Growing up legalistic in the 1950s, I acquired a different phobia for every hour of the day. Men and women grow up with less stringent standards now, and Dave might not have seen any problem in being alone with the woman in her car. I was probably overreacting.

And it might not even have been Dave.

The guy was half a block away. I only saw him for a few seconds, and I never got a clear view of his face. Maybe he just looked like Dave.

I cleared my desk and packed to go home. Slipping on my blazer, I checked my gig line, tugged down my cuffs, and came to a realization. *That guy couldn't have been Dave. He was dressed up.*

This had been a sore point with me, and I was surprised I hadn't thought of it sooner. Dave and his untucked T-shirts and his shorts and his Birkenstocks. I had thought it unprofessional for a pastor to show up for work that way. It had to affect his attitude. When the casual Friday thing started, my employees went giddy and teased each other about how they looked. Next thing I knew, they were missing obvious signs of forgery and check kiting—and they weren't balancing their tills.

I tried not to let Dave's juvenile appearance irritate me. But he knew how to wear a coat and tie on Sundays. Why couldn't he do button-downs the rest of the week? Still had a streak of the youth pastor in him, I guess.

Anyway, the guy who had gotten out of the woman's car had worn a sport coat and khakis. That was not Dave on a Tuesday afternoon. Maybe the fact that it wasn't his car and it wasn't his wife and it wasn't his clothes meant it wasn't Dave.

I ambled through the empty bank.

And even if Dave *were* the guy getting out of that car, if he was doing something really bad, like having an affair, would it make sense for him to have his mistress drop him off at the Bean? That would be the last place he'd go with her.

Dave was always at the Bean. He met people there and studied there almost every day. He knew I went there. He knew I could see the Bean from my office window. In fact, he and I would watch from my window as guys from the church drove in for their discipleship appointments.

Dave was no dummy. If there was one thing I'd learned about him, it was that in any situation he knew what people would think and how they would react. He could foresee what was going to set people off and he'd give them a kind of vaccination to ward off the problem.

At one congregational meeting, one of the trustees, Mike, was describing how we were going to renovate the basement. This was one of his soapbox issues, and the more he talked, the more excited he got. He'd wanted the renovation for a long time because of the carpet, which he said was "awful." He'd used that word in every committee meeting we'd had on the renovation. He didn't mean that the carpet had become awful over twenty years, but that it had been awful even as a show-room sample.

I wasn't listening real close because I already knew the details. I wasn't listening, that is, until Mike made his reference to the "awful carpet," and then my spine froze. Agnes Thurman, a stalwart supporter of the church, had made a point to attend that meeting. And Agnes's late husband had chosen the basement carpet. Panic. It's one thing if a great carpet wears out. But it's another thing if your carpet choice has merely been endured as a tribulation that worketh patience.

I looked to where Agnes was seated in the back, and Dave was already there. He'd been there for a while, in fact, quietly talking and laughing with her, so that when Mike said "awful carpet," she didn't even hear it. She didn't see people stealing glances at her, either. The pastor was talking with her, and that was all she knew.

Dave had predicted that Mike would say the word *awful*. He was way ahead of everybody else.

Was this the sort of guy to forget that I could see the Bean's front door from my office? Or that I could study the faces of drivers as they went by my window?

I felt I should give Dave the benefit of the doubt. It was ridiculous to imagine that he was in sin with this woman. He wasn't that stupid.

And it probably wasn't him anyway.

I got as far toward home as sliding my key into the ignition when I realized I'd left my sunglasses in the office. It was at moments like this I was sorry I'd ever started wearing them. At first, I'd needed them in the late afternoons because the sun blinded me as I drove home. Once I got used to that, I started wearing them in the mornings as I drove to work, even though the sun wasn't nearly as bright. Then I wore them every sunny day. Pretty soon, I was wearing them continuously—even on cloudy days, because of "the glare."

Pathetic. I'm addicted to my sunglasses.

I pulled my key out of the slot, walked back to the bank, unlocked the door, punched my code into the alarm system, unlocked my office, and got my sunglasses.

After locking my office, reentering my code, and relocking the front door, I turned and started to walk back to my car. More out of habit than anything else, I glanced down the street toward the Bean. Just at that moment, out the front door walked the sport coat and khakis. The guy's head turned in my direction, and he waved from half a block away. It was Dave.

Timing is a funny thing.

If I hadn't forgotten my sunglasses—even if I'd remembered them at any other moment—I wouldn't have seen Dave walking out of the Bean. I would've gone with the evidence at hand and concluded that he'd never been in that car. No anxiety. No confrontations. No board meeting.

Instead, I saw that it was indeed Dave, and now I had an issue that wasn't going to go away.

Like I said, timing is a funny thing.

Back in the car, with the traffic guy shouting his report because I'd forgotten to turn the radio down after lunch, I watched Dave drive off in his Rabbit and clenched my jaw. I had to start over with this problem. I tried to evict my frustration with a sigh and then whipped onto McKinley, forcing a deliveryman to stand on his brakes.

There are nineteen stoplights between the bank and home. Twenty years ago, we'd built our house at that location so I'd always be able to fly to work along the edge of town. This would be the last housing development for a while, we'd told ourselves. No one else would move here. Not to our town. I realized my country lane had gone suburban when they wired the fifth intersection. Now it was four times worse.

The more stoplights, the more your car marked your status in our newly divided town. Now you started noticing the lawyers in their Beamers, and the doctors and real estate agents in their Mercedes or Cadillacs. The teachers drove Hondas with politically instructive bumper stickers, and there was no shortage of Infinitis, Lexuses, and Audis. In time we saw our first Hummer—and then it seemed like everyone was driving one. Even the down-and-outers became upwardly mobile. They'd buy a worn-out Lexus and fix the broken lights with duct tape.

My Camry may have been vanilla, but it was clean.

My daughter's Saturn was another matter. Washing it made me wince. All I saw were the hundred-dollar abrasions and the parking-lot dings. The dark green finish showed each speck of dirt like it was part of a prize collection. Those cars only looked good the first year. After that, all the sun-bleached plastic appeared as if it would crumple if you leaned on it. Rachel's sedan was three years old. No matter how often I washed it, it still looked like the bargain from repo purgatory that it was. She needed something else.

Rachel was my prize for getting the big things right. Even if the bank went under and we lost our house, I would've felt successful because of her. She was seventeen and still smiling. She was more than a good kid; she'd blossomed into a young woman with both smarts and popularity. To watch her navigate the relational straits of adolescence was far more satisfying than scanning earnings reports. I listened to her on the phone with her friends like she was singing my favorite song. She had grace and beauty and compassion.

Then there was Audrey. Because every workday included ten hours of uptight women, what I looked forward to most at 6 PM was the sight of my wife's face. She usually wore the same expression as the first time I saw her; a look of satisfied amusement, as if the guy gaping at her with admiration had just ridden his bike into a tree. Which in fact, I had. The years had added lines that only deepened the laughter in her gray eyes and intensified my fascination.

By the sixth stoplight, I had recovered enough objectivity to return to the problem of the woman in the Mercedes.

I needed to err on the side of grace. Dave wouldn't have been in the woman's car without a very good reason. I considered his ministry—all the good he had done in his seven years as pastor and the sincerity he displayed in his life. Though I'd had many frustrations with Dave, I could say for certain he was not a fake. In the pulpit, he didn't get up and display his knowledge of theological trivia every week. He was a real guy, with no pretense that he had it all together. Maybe his stories about the wild parties in college before he got saved made people uncomfortable. Maybe he gave too much detail about the kegs and the girls. But at least you knew he wasn't a legalist.

He could be very persuasive. I still remembered the time he preached from 1 Thessalonians 4:3—"For this is the will of God, even your sanctification, that ye should abstain from fornication." He probably quoted from *The Message*, but my default version is still the King James, because I memorized verses—lots of verses—from it when I was a kid. In Sunday school in 1967, I got a prize for memorizing all of Psalm 90. It was the only time I ever saw my dad's eyes well up.

In his sermon Dave had said we all struggle to know God's will for our daily lives, but we make it too complicated. The verse in Thessalonians tells us what God's will is. Sexual purity. Dave talked about why this is God's very best plan for us. He described the costs of immorality—the diseases, the unwanted pregnancies, the loss of self-worth. Immorality is unhealthy, he said. He'd laid it out straight. I remembered thinking, *This is what church is all about. The young people really need to hear this, and they won't hear it anywhere else.*

At the end of the sermon, he'd given an invitation. Any of the kids who wanted to pursue God's very best could come forward. I guess lots of kids went. But I only saw Rachel, who got up silently and swiftly, without making eye contact with Audrey or me. Hurried little steps down the aisle. Her back curled forward as she knelt at the platform steps. Red-rimmed eyes when she came back. It was the first time she'd made a spiritual decision apart from parental influence, and it stuck. All through high school so far, she'd only gone on group dates. She read books about traditional courtship. She was many times more cautious than I had been at her age.

Dave's preaching did have its problems. Most Sundays, it wasn't my cup of tea, with all the stories and the tear-jerking personal experiences. On more than one occasion, I had pressed him to put more Bible in his sermons. But regardless, he was genuine. I had to give him that.

And then there was his family.

Derek and Amanda were not your typical PKs, with the attitude and the secret rebellion—secret from the parents, anyway. These two were under control. They were affectionate. They were kind, always including other kids in whatever they did. I once saw Derek—he couldn't have been more than seven at the time—help one of the three-year-olds down the stairs to the church basement. Held the little guy's hand and stayed with him, each unbearably slow step of the way. Kindness and patience are not things boys have in their DNA. They have to be trained.

Dave's wife, Amy—well, she was some kind of angelic servant. Hardly ever said a word, but she had a calming warmth about her. We were in Dave and Amy's home pretty often, and even though it wasn't the most orderly place—lots of toys on the floor, little stacks of magazines and mail around, plates and glasses left on the coffee table—it was comfortable. I liked it there. With Amy, you were always welcome. There was your favorite soda. There was a brownie that five-year-old Amanda had helped bake. There were stools in the kitchen, where you could sit at the counter while Amy went about whatever she was doing, as if you were just another member of the family.

The day that Audrey found out she had breast cancer, Amy came over. Didn't ask. She just came. She sat my wife down in our kitchen and listened to her talk for three hours. While she listened, she made dinner for my family. Audrey is a very together woman. Amy gave her time to feel the blow.

I had some reservations about the way Dave handled his family, but it was hard to argue with the results. He seemed to have a temper, and I'd seen him yell at the kids once or twice out of embarrassment at their behavior, but those were quibbles. Dave's family was alive. In my book that made him real.

I think what had impressed me most about Dave, even beyond his family, was his gracious attitude—which I had seen in living color when my dad died.

Dad was my highest model for godliness. He was unmatched in his discipline and devotion. After his funeral, I had snagged the King James Bible he had used when I was growing up, and I still do my daily reading from it. Even after decades of use, when I picked it up from the corner of his desk, it was in pristine condition—the binding intact, the leather supple, the pages neatly marked with brackets and dates, yet smooth.

But for all his godly character, Dad had been a thorn in the side of every pastor I could remember. If you got him off by himself, he was pretty reasonable. He could see the other guy's point of view, he could shoot the breeze, and he was a funny storyteller. But there was something about church meetings, especially ones that dealt with the budget. As a CPA, he knew rules and regulations that almost nobody else had even heard of. While roll was taken or the minutes from the last meeting were read, he'd comb through the financials, and you could feel the heat from his face. Once the floor was open for discussion, Dad would let the board have it with both barrels. This or that fund was unethical. The program income accounts were padded. All he'd ever seen in the church was impropriety in reporting. That sort of thing. It seemed to come from professional pride. He was a trustee only once.

When I was a boy, Pastor Schneider had gotten so mad at one of Dad's outbursts that he'd stalked out and written his resignation. A delegation had to leave the meeting and persuade him to tear it up. And Pastor Beck, after some meetings, wouldn't speak to Dad for weeks. He'd see Dad coming up the line for a handshake after the service and he'd bound off after some other guy, as if he'd forgotten to tell him something.

Dave had never seemed to have a problem with Dad. In fact, he went out of his way to consult him, even after Dad, in the heat of the moment at a congregational meeting—in front of everyone—told Dave to read *Accounting for Dummies*.

Years ago I swore I would never hold my professional expertise over the church like a mallet. But Dave just seemed to take my dad's behavior in stride.

Anyway, when Dave did the funeral for Dad, he gave a eulogy that amazed me. He did the usual thing of reminding us of Dad's funny stories, and he remarked about Dad's dedication to the church over the years. But he didn't stop there. He also told how Dad had done his taxes every year for free; how the money Dad had saved him paid for family vacations. He told how Dad walked him through the purchase of a home and personally planted a tree in the back yard as a reminder of God's faithfulness. He never referred to any of Dad's less attractive characteristics—not even lightly or in fun. As far as you knew from that eulogy, Dad's sharp tongue didn't exist.

It was the most gracious act I'd ever seen. None of our other pastors would've spoken that way. And none of them had put in the time with Dad that Dave had.

Yes, I'd had my frustrations with Dave—and about more than his weekday wardrobe. But those tensions were normal, I guess. We'd always wondered about our pastors, so wondering about this one didn't seem out of the ordinary. Pastors are rarely an ideal fit for a congregation, and ours were no exception. Church business had a way of drawing the battle lines, and we rarely saw much wisdom in our pastors' grand schemes.

But now, even with the tensions, things were tangibly improving. We had bought land for a new facility—a lot of land, too, in a growing part of town. The perennial fights had died down. Dave had stuck it out through some tough personality conflicts and misunderstandings, and the whole body was better for it. We were overcoming the trials.

At stoplight nineteen, I decided I didn't need to ask Dave about the woman.

2

I had analyzed our neighborhood's traffic patterns long ago, looking for the optimum route home. The thicket of avenues and cul-de-sacs offered many challenges to my driving technique. There were tight bends, one roundabout near the elementary school, and a sharp right leading to a meandering uphill climb. I developed two approaches for negotiating the course—one for preserving my passengers' sense of security, and another for when I was driving alone. I hoped one day to get all the way to the house without dropping below 15 mph.

Today was dismal. Some obvious newcomer was stopped at the roundabout, and there was an open house at the school. Bowed but unbroken, I glided along the winding route to our street.

Our house compared favorably with the neighbors' because I maintained a high standard. I kept the paint fresh, the bushes clean, and the lawn plush. Now that my trees had matured, I associated them with the Impressionist prints that Audrey had hung in the living room—especially seeing the leaves at

38 mph. The trees shielded my view from the increasing number of rental properties, with their peeling paint and rotting fences. But the trees could only hide so much. Renters decorate with junk. The tenants next door inflicted their seasonal lawn ornaments on the neighborhood—like the Santa whose arm had been severed and reattached with duct tape. But at least it was red duct tape.

Not that our home didn't have its own issues. I brooded over them each time I drove up, especially this evening.

Defacing a length of curb out front was Rachel's Saturn, glistening with drips of sap. The closer I came, the tighter my lips compressed. She had parked or driven too close to some sprinkler, and it had sprayed over the hood, dissolving the sap into blotches of film. The left rear tire was scraped from some misjudged parallel-parking attempt. And the vacuum seal on my day's coffin: the windshield now sported a new zit, an obnoxiously symmetrical bull's-eye precisely in the driver's line of sight, with a crack pushing out to the edge of the glass.

I thumb-punched the garage door opener.

In the kitchen, I found Rachel leaning against the counter, sipping lemonade as if nothing had happened. "Hi, Dad!"

"What happened to your windshield?"

"Windshield?" She set down her lemonade.

"You got a huge crack in your windshield. When did it happen?"

"I don't know, Dad. I didn't even see it."

"What do you mean you didn't see it? It's right in your line of sight."

"I was driving, not inspecting the glass. I just didn't see it."

"You have to look through the glass to drive. When something breaks the glass, it interferes with your driving. And then you notice."

She looked away and folded her arms. "I obviously should've seen it, then."

"Yes, you should've. I still don't understand why you didn't."

"We can get it fixed, right?"

I flipped through the mail. "No, we can't 'get it fixed.' The whole windshield will have to be replaced."

She looked at the floor. "I'm sorry. I'll pay for it."

"You'll pay for it? How much do you think a windshield costs?"

"Dad, I don't know. I've never bought one before. You always take the car to the shop, not me. I don't even know what it costs to have the oil filtered."

"Changed. You change oil."

"Whatever. I'm just saying I've got some money saved."

"What money?"

"For a prom dress."

"You've got three hundred dollars?"

"Two hundred."

"A windshield costs over three."

Her shoulders sagged. "Okay, I'll pay back the rest. It might take a while."

"Well, cars cost a lot of money, Rachel. I've put a lot into the Saturn already."

"I'm sorry, Dad. I said I'll pay for it. But I don't even know how I broke it."

I looked up from the mail. "How could you not know? You were driving along. You heard a very loud smack. And there in your line of sight was a fresh bull's-eye. It happens when you tailgate."

"Dad—"

"Well, weren't you tailgating?"

My bellowing was a poor habit. I usually recognized I was doing it a nanosecond before Audrey appeared. And here she was now, right on schedule.

"No, Dad, I was not tailgating."

I turned away and took off my jacket. "Well, the next time it sounds like a bullet hit your car, notice."

I looked at Audrey. She didn't have the amused expression I was hoping for. But she kissed me. "Welcome home. Bad day?"

"No, just typical."

Rachel sighed and grabbed her lemonade. "Yeah."

Audrey looked at us. "Okay, so we're not off to a good start." She patted my shoulder. "You go change. You're not ready for more women. Rachel, would you slice the tomatoes for me, please? I'll get some enchiladas in the oven and we'll try the family thing again later." She gave me a firm but nonviolent push toward the master bedroom.

After a couple of minutes of muffled voices, Audrey came in and shut the door. "Got a call from Amy a little while ago. She was just saying hi. Nothing special. But I thought the background noise was hilarious. Dave gets home while Amy's talking and the kids explode. I can hear Derek yelling and Amanda squealing and Dave growling like a bear. Then they're all laughing so loud I can't hear Amy anymore, so we hang up. Our pastor's wild."

"Yeah, the kids love him," I said. I could smell the setup.

"Daddy getting home is the high point of the day."

That wasn't it. Still part of the setup. Audrey was good.

She folded some towels, which meant I was toast. Some women knit to create an ominous atmosphere, like the French woman in one of those Dickens stories. Some women throw plates, and others go silent. Audrey folds towels.

"Rachel got some good news today."

"Yeah?"

"She was excited."

"What was it?"

"She wants to tell you herself." One towel, folded and set on the bedspread.

"I'll have to ask her."

"Yep."

"Something to do with her classes?"

"Her classes don't get her that excited." Two towels.

"Don't tell me she's got a boyfriend—or whatever it is she calls a guy she wants to court."

"She was chattering on the phone with her friends like she'd won the lotto."

"I'm starting to doubt how good this news is."

"She was waiting in the kitchen for you to get home." Three towels.

I put up my hands preemptively. "I get it. I trampled on her good news with the windshield thing. I disappointed her. But I couldn't have known about the news."

"You could've chosen a better time for the windshield than when you first walked in the door."

"I'll make it up to her. But she's got to learn what things cost."

Four towels. "I agree. But wouldn't she learn better from something that was actually her fault?"

I filled the pockets of my jeans.

"I seem to recall you picking up your share of window cracks."

Wallet, hanky, antacids.

"And the tailgating thing was pretty rich, Jim, especially coming from you."

Five towels.

"I think you owe her an apology."

A five-towel confrontation was far from the most excruciating I'd endured. But still, the message was clear. I had to stop bellowing.

Audrey slipped back out to finish dinner, leaving me to grieve my sins.

Instead, my mind seized on the part about Dave, Amy, and their kids, and I resumed brooding about the woman in the Mercedes.

Was there a problem here? Granted, I didn't want there to be a problem. But was there a problem, regardless of whether I wanted one? Regardless of the land purchase, and the building campaign, and the feeling that our church was finally getting past all the usual garbage to some real ministry? Setting all that completely aside, was there a problem here?

Yes, in the sense that my pastor was in the car with her, alone. It looked bad.

But no, in the sense that Dave couldn't really be guilty of something. If he were in sin, I continued to think, he would've avoided being seen with the woman at his main hangout—and he never would have waved at me. Guilty people hide. Adam and Eve hid from the Lord and sewed fig leaves together to cover themselves when they sinned. Achan buried the spoils he'd stolen from Jericho. Men in their offices look over their shoulders when they pull up Internet porn.

Dave wasn't hiding.

Of course, he might just be shameless. He was pretty smart about people. He could've bet that it was safer to sin in the open, because people only question what appears secretive.

The possibility interested me as I ran the shaver over my face. Could my pastor commit adultery in the open, trusting that no one would catch on? What would he have to do to get such confidence? Was he capable of playing this game?

I ran the scenario.

First, he gets comfortable teaching one thing in the pulpit and doing the opposite when the sermon is over. He preaches a sermon about purity, like the one he did from 1 Thessalonians, with so much passion that we buy it, but without being so persuasive that he convicts himself. He leaves loopholes.

Then he cuts all the strings of responsibility and feeling tying him to his family. He gets comfortable talking to his wife as if nothing's wrong. He can look at his kids without feeling guilty.

Actually, he turns his back on the whole church, abandons all the love he's invested in the body. He calculates the chances of exposure, and figures the consequences for all the people he's counseled, baptized, and taught. And after doing the spiritual cost-benefit analysis, he says, "It's worth it."

But all that only gets him into the adultery itself. How does he get to the point of sinning openly?

I guess he experiments with people's stupidity. There's no way he can be so straightforward without taking smaller risks and getting away with them. He tests the effect of a church member seeing him at an R-rated movie. How do the interactions go? Is he challenged? Are there any consequences at all? Truth is, there probably aren't. He climbs the ladder of risk from there. Can he be seen in a bar or smoking a cigar without any consequences? Only after he had successfully experimented could he be seen at the Bean with his mistress and act like nothing strange had happened.

That was a lot of sin to contemplate. Dave would have to lie, conspire against his family and his congregation, and assault their moral courage. I didn't think he was capable of committing so many sins. Sin would have to reside in his very heart, just waiting to get out, for him to do so many terrible things. And I knew Dave had a good heart.

By the time I slathered aftershave over my cheeks, I felt the speculations were idle, even theological. I only indulged them as a kind of exercise, having already made my decision. I didn't need to ask Dave about the woman.

It was time to put matters back on track with Rachel.

I sat down to chips and salsa and waited for an opening while Rachel and Audrey put the finishing touches on dinner. I smiled. I made appreciative noises. "Great salsa." I complimented the lemonade. Each time they returned to the table with a dish, I made sure they knew how delicious it smelled. Now Audrey's amused expression was back.

But Rachel wasn't softening. No eye contact. No smile. No acknowledgment of my presence, trip after trip. She brought the enchiladas at last. "You must've made those, Rachel." She pulled her lips tight, looking steadfastly at the dish. The tolerant face. I'd really ticked her off this time.

"Great salsa. Boy! That fresh cilantro really makes the difference."

I kept my dinnertime prayer even more general than usual and tore into the food. "How did school go today, Rachel?"

"Fine."

"That's good." Some thoughtful chewing. "What was fine about it?"

"Nothing."

I suppressed my usual comeback. "So, nothing unusual happened?"

"Nothing unusual ever happens."

"Oh." More thoughtful chewing. "So school was boring."

"It was fine."

"What about after school. Was that fine too?"

"Yeah."

I looked at Audrey, who smiled at her black beans.

"Great enchiladas. Wow!"

The evening trudged into the late hours. I set the TV remote aside and looked at the light from Rachel's doorway. She was still doing homework. I knew what I had to say.

"Rachel?"

She looked up from her biology book.

"I'll pay for the windshield."

"Thanks, Dad." Finally, a bit of warmth.

"You're welcome."

"I'm sorry I broke it."

3

Flynn shuffled her notes from our review of Melissa. "And now, your favorite."

"My favorite? They're all my favorites."

"Mm-hmm." Her smile had a touch of smirk at the corners. "So what do you mean, *favorite*?"

"Some are more favorite than others." She flicked a glance at me over the rim of her glasses.

"She's a special favorite?"

"You're only human."

"So I've got a thing for Melissa now."

"I didn't say that. I merely observe."

"Observe what?"

"You're awfully attentive."

I rolled my eyes. "I'm attentive to all our employees."

"Yeah, but you've never noticed *my* white knuckles."

"Hmm. Didn't know liberated women could be jealous."

The smirk turned ever so slightly scornful.

I sat a little taller. "Melissa has some problems. I'm attentive to that."

"She definitely has problems."

"What, you think I'm shielding her?"

Flynn's eyes played behind a renewed poker face. "You protect all the employees. Even me."

"Yes, even you. When you became head teller, you couldn't coordinate the schedules of four turtles."

Flynn smiled and looked over toward the window. "You taught us everything we know."

"I let you cover shifts for a month. Never even wrote you up."

"I was grateful."

"Of course you were. You learned the importance of scheduling."

"We owe our lives to you. Can't we get on with this?"

"Of course."

She tossed her hair back and scanned her notes. "I commended her for customer service and sales. But I wrote her up for not balancing and for inappropriate attire. No formal warning. Just some steps for improvement."

"Very good."

"Never throw a person away." Another glance.

"Exactly. Melissa was probably expecting a first warning. You watch—she'll work smarter."

"Mm-hmm." Flynn straightened her notes. "So are we done here?"

For the rest of the afternoon, "working smarter" was not how I would have described myself. I read memos two and three times. I sat in front of a white computer screen with the stationary cursor nagging at me. I pulled up Drudge. I checked my e-mail every ten minutes. I knew this condition well, but I was always slow to recognize it. Inability to focus, lethargy, new-idea retardation. These symptoms meant I'd neglected some duty in the past twenty-four hours but was unwilling to admit it.

I usually acknowledged the situation when I started feeling like I was twelve years old again and trying to justify the deck of cards in my backpack to my mother.

Mom was the Meryl Streep of guilt. I've never met anyone with her powers to express disappointment. The right side of her mouth tugged slightly outward, like a suppressed wince. Her eyes darkened and grew round. She carried that look for days sometimes, leaving me to figure out what I'd done wrong—or whether it was even meant for me. Mom knew that tiny gestures carried force.

Her powers of expression extended beyond the grave. Even now, years after her death, and almost four decades since I was twelve, she stared at me from inside my brain, the right corner of her mouth pulling outward. More than that, she was able to gather the strength of other people's expectations into her service. I had to justify every negligence to Flynn, the girls, Audrey, Rachel, whomever—not because they demanded it, but because Mom winced. I felt I could either make excuses in a pinched voice or be heartless and blow off the people I should care for the most.

On this afternoon, Mom mustered the entire congregation to her banner, hundreds of Baptists. Like it or not, I had a responsibility to the church. *I'm the church chairman, for Pete's sake.*

I saw those two Bean kids on their break again, and my mind shifted back to yesterday. They had grinned over Dave's ride in the Mercedes—looked at each other and grinned. I saw them. I knew what it meant.

Those two kids were laughing at the church. Dave had given them an opening to think he was a hypocrite, and now the kids were laughing. They were telling their friends about the hypocrite pastor at the Baptist church.

Even though I'd seen them laughing, I had decided—consciously decided—not to say anything to Dave. I, the chairman of the board of trustees. Such a disappointment.

I seized a pencil and started whacking it on the edge of the desk. I took a deep breath and blew the air out through my teeth. If Audrey were here, she would've laid her fingertips on my knee to stop it from bouncing. I scratched out a heading—"Scenarios"—on a yellow pad, one I kept at hand for replacing thought with activity.

More whacking with the pencil.

The coffee guys could've been grinning about Dave's clothes. They were used to seeing him in T-shirts and Birkenstocks. Maybe his sudden formality was funny. I underlined *Scenarios* and added "Weird Clothes."

But the funny thing could've been the car, not just Dave's clothes. The T-shirt guy who drives a Rabbit suddenly emerges in a sport coat from a Mercedes. After all, they kept looking back at the car. "Status Jump."

This didn't mean they saw the woman. They probably couldn't see the driver like I could. For all they knew, the driver was a man. It was possible they reacted only to the car. "No Woman."

These scenarios were plausible enough to fortify me against taking the matter to the congregation. Except for two things.

The raised eyebrows. Even from half a block away, their expressions flashed "Gotcha!" Even before I saw the woman, I felt the impact of those raised eyebrows. I couldn't ignore the guys' perception that they'd caught a pastor doing something he shouldn't. It didn't matter what they thought Dave was doing, or whether he was guilty or innocent; they thought ill of the church.

Beyond even that, I couldn't ignore that I was having to work so hard to forget what I'd seen. Why was I coming up with so many excuses for Dave? None of them altered the fact that he was in a car, alone, with a woman who wasn't his wife.

I reversed my decision. Dave lacked maturity and judgment, and I needed to talk to him. I'd pop over and see him before dinner.

I tossed the pencil back into its leather-wrapped cup and went out to see the girls.

Flynn glanced at the clock and slid papers across her desk for a new customer to sign. Tammy, the drive-up teller, was saying a melodic bye-bye to her last customer, after getting a doggy biscuit for the man's slobbering golden retriever. The owner of the video rental store across the parking lot was flirting with Crystal, who counted his cash and surveyed his paunch.

I strolled over to Melissa. She must've heard my shoes clapping the tile, because she turned and beamed. Between her manicured fingers was a beautiful sheet of paper with balancing numbers.

I gave her a thumbs-up. "Perfect."

She whisked her hair behind her ear. "I even have ten minutes to spare."

She was working smarter already. And no cleavage.

I returned to my office to find Flynn with papers for me to initial. She leaned over my yellow pad, the back of her hand on her hip. "Scenarios: weird clothes, status jump, and no woman. You going out tonight?"

I frowned. "No such luck. I've got a meeting."

She handed me the papers while still looking at the pad, a lock of hair suspended by her cheek. "What sort of meeting? I've got to see you in these weird clothes."

I said nothing, just scratched my initials on the pages.

Flynn's voice changed. "Seriously, Jim, you haven't been yourself this afternoon. Is something wrong?"

I handed the papers back without looking at her. "I'm on my way to find out."

I drove to Dave's house and realized on the way that I'd never tracked a guy down to tell him he needed to look after himself. And the more I imagined doing it, the less I knew what I had to tell him. Be smarter? Or be better?

If you tell a guy to be smarter, you're saying he has to manage himself more effectively so he doesn't get into trouble. Usually you're saying he's naïve. "Don't just pull over and help that guy lying on the ground! He can turn around and sue you. Wise up!"

Did Dave need to be smarter? Definitely. To ride alone with that woman in her Mercedes was at least naïve, especially for a man in his position.

But if you tell a guy to be better, you're making another statement altogether. You're saying he has poor character. You're not talking so much about what he does as about who he is—his thoughts and motivations. You're going deeper than telling him to be more mature. You're almost attacking his manliness, and no matter how you try to be specific, you can't escape the implication that he's a bad person.

Did Dave need to be better? Was I going to tell my pastor he lacked integrity?

I didn't know.

Jesus said, "Judge not, that ye be not judged." But when I was growing up, it seemed the church's motto was, "Judge *first*, that ye be not judged."

They judged people who smoked and drank and played cards. Dancers and moviegoers were under the ban too, as were men who wore long hair, women who wore pants, and boys who wore blue shirts to church. Those were just the prohibitions. The duties were worse. You didn't just memorize verses; you memorized the Shakespearean English of the KJV, and you got every word right or you were unfaithful to the Word of God. You didn't merely attend Sunday services; you faced forward with your feet flat on the floor and refrained from blinking. When my best friend got baptized, Pastor Beck left the very front hairs of his flat-top dry. His dad made the pastor do it again.

The Christian life of my childhood was full of reminders that people were bad. I'd rejected that kind of churchianity long ago, and had made it a goal to do church graciously. No more throwing people away.

So what would give me the right to judge Dave and say he needed to be better? Nothing, as far as I could see—especially not on the flimsy basis of a car ride with a woman.

I would tell Dave to be smarter, then. But how?

I could put on the attitude I used at the bank. Sit him down. Smile real big. "We've got a little problem, Dave, and I thought I'd just ask what we could do to solve it." Use open gestures. Be concrete. Don't generalize. "I saw you get out of a gal's car yesterday." Concerned sounding. "I was kind of wondering what the explanation for that might be." Or, "Do you think it was the wisest thing to ride with her like that?"

The problem was, I wasn't Dave's boss. He was my pastor. I couldn't talk to him like I was getting down on his level to help. The pastor's over the chairman, no matter what. I'd seen other chairmen talk down to pastors. Stupid.

I could put on the attitude of an older man—world-weary, seen it all. "Dave, trust me, what may seem small at your stage of life, riding with that woman, has huge repercussions." Then explain from experience. "I've seen pastors walk a thin line between propriety and impropriety, and let me tell you, it's—"

Except I hadn't seen this before. Ever. I'd never had to itemize what propriety was or wasn't, because I'd never seen one of our pastors alone with a woman who wasn't his wife, under any circumstances. And if I was inexperienced in that sort of thing, how was I supposed to play the older, wiser man?

Maybe there was no sense approaching the issue as an authority figure. Maybe authority would just complicate matters.

I could approach him as a brother. Point both hands toward my heart. Shake my head. "Don't get me wrong, Dave. I need Jesus too. I've got issues." Minimize. "I'm not saying you committed one of the seven deadly sins, but . . ." Ask a perspective-setting question. "If you saw me doing something that wasn't smart, what would you do, as my brother?"

But I didn't believe any of that. What did it matter if I had issues in my life? I didn't have this issue. Minimize what I saw? I'd been trying to do that for a whole day. Dumb is dumb. It's irreducible. If approaching Dave as a brother meant acting like what he did wasn't dumb, then brotherliness wasn't going to work.

These quandaries began to seem adolescent. Wasn't confrontation one of life's basic skills? Didn't I do this with my daughter? Didn't I do it at work? No one ever succeeded in business without confrontation. Why was this time so confusing?

I decided to use a time-honored masculine strategy for problem-solving.

Wing it.

Dave had been home for a while by the time I got to his house. The Rabbit was no longer clicking as it sat in the driveway. I could hear shrieks of children's laughter from inside the house. Some savory casserole was in the oven.

The front yard looked like a domestic explosion. I walked past overturned tricycles, little cars and trucks scattered about, dolls lying in various contortions, tiny shoes cast across the lawn. Flip-flops lay jumbled where Amy had sat, her magazine blown into a corner of the patio. There were two abandoned plastic cups rolling around as if they'd been knocked off the rail, red juice dribbling out. The front door swung on its hinges. The noise of play echoed over the abandoned mess.

I stood in the doorway unobserved for a while, content to listen to sounds that had ceased in my own home. Then I tried to make my presence known. "Knock, knock!"

Amy appeared, wiping her hands with a towel. "Hi, Jim! Sorry we didn't hear you. It's pretty noisy." She led me into the kitchen and offered me something to drink, then went to find Dave.

My pastor emerged with Amanda dangling from his arm like a chimp, screaming and laughing. She was looking up at his face, oblivious to everyone else. Derek was crawling back and forth between Dave's feet, growling and throwing his shoulder against his father's calves. Dave was sweaty. There had already been a lot of play.

I asked if I could talk to him for a bit (already minimizing), and we went to his office.

I'd been in this tiny room before, but for some reason I'd never noticed how orderly it was. The desk was spotless; no stacks, no leftover work, no mug with a brown ring in the bottom. The writing pad was centered in front of the chair, as if the space had been measured. Three holders that matched the pad were lined up by height along the far edge—one for pencils, all sharp, another for pens, all different colors but the same brand and type, and a third for paper clips. The three cups were exactly the same distance apart, and the grouping was centered between an immaculately white computer monitor and a pair of stacking trays that matched the holders and the pad. Nothing was in the trays—not even dust.

The room smelled like Pledge.

My eye went to the baseboard, which had been painted, nailed to the wall, and the nail holes filled and touched up, all with unbelievable precision. The carpet looked as if it had been vacuumed five minutes ago. The wall, which I knew to have been painted several years ago, looked fresh. The outside of the door was scratched, chipped, and marked. But when Dave shut it, I looked at the inside. Pristine.

The only sign of disorder, if it could be called that, was a strategy game that Dave had set up on a little side table. It was one of those complicated military board games, designed to represent the details of an old battle. This one looked like Waterloo, with Napoleon's army represented by a bunch of little cardboard squares in formation at one end of the board— the squares notated with troop strengths—and Wellington's army at the other.

I nodded to the table. "I thought only eggheads played these games."

Dave smiled and shrugged as we sat down on opposite sides of the board.

4

Judging from their statues, the Romans had a graceful gesture for getting people's attention: they reached out with a downturned palm. The King James Bible has a rich "O" to use when it wants to grab you: "Bless the Lord, O my soul!" Shakespeare used something I had thought was catchy when I was in high school: "How now! What news?" And it was about the only thing of Shakespeare I'd understood.

We have the word *um*. It starts most meetings and conversations, though a close second would be "Okay!" *Um* begins almost every impromptu speech: "Um, I just wanted to say . . ." It can also be a transition in private conversation from talking about sports or cars to a potentially inflammatory issue: "Um, I was wondering . . . what happened to that chainsaw I loaned you last fall?"

Um is a gesture of modesty we think wins people over. I can't account for it otherwise. *Um* has no meaning. It doesn't reach out. It doesn't even sound good. It's just a little tic to use when you're expected to take the initiative and look self-conscious at the same time.

And when you're venturing into a confrontation without a clear rationale or goal, as I was, the urge to lower expectations is primal.

But I didn't have to open. Instead, Dave's eyebrows plunged, and he said, "Um, can I ask you something?"

"Sure, Dave."

"Are you here about the gal who dropped me off yesterday?"

"Um—"

"Look, I'm totally comfortable being confronted about something like that. In fact, it's a real encouragement to me. You came all the way over here to ask about the gal, and I respect that. Most guys would let the issue slide. But you've always been committed to accountability. That means a lot to me."

"Yeah, well, I just couldn't help but wonder."

"Sure. Anybody would. But not everybody would pursue it. I guess that's why you're finally chairman, Jim. People know you're about getting things right. You'll make sure we're on the straight and narrow."

"Well, that's nice of you to say. But I don't want you to think I always imagine the worst—"

"Getting things right is really important. More people need to be like you, watching out for others."

"—because I don't. I actually try to think the best."

"If more guys held their brothers accountable, we'd have a lot more openness."

"Yeah, but I don't want you to think that's all I care about—"

Dave held up his hands. "Oh, no—no, Jim. I know you. You care about people."

"Or that I'm watching you all the time, waiting for a slip-up."

"No, I understand."

"I mean, I know what it's been like for you and the other pastors here. So many people being negative. It seems like everybody's had a pet issue he's determined to fight over. Mike and the basement. Dad and the books. I don't want any part of that."

Dave leaned forward slightly. "I see that in you. I know your heart. That's why I don't mind being accountable to you. I'm in safe hands. So what did you want to ask me? Fire away."

That was what I admired about Dave from the first day he was pastor. He was open. Maybe he had a lot to learn. Maybe his immaturity got him in trouble. But he had the ability to confront problems, even when they were his own. His attitude always seemed humble, as if he were learning from me. That was gratifying. But I often felt like I was learning from him.

Still, I had to think fast, because now I was in a bind. He had volunteered the fact that he'd ridden with the woman without necessarily knowing why I'd come over. If I'd come about something else, this would've amounted to a pretty serious confession—a confession he wouldn't have had to make. He wouldn't throw away security if he were guilty of something major. Wasn't my question answered? Did I really need to hear the details?

I decided this was my opening to be straight with him. "I guess my main concern is that riding with a woman who's not your wife—in her Mercedes like that, alone—well, it just isn't real smart. It opens up all sorts of problems, no matter how reasonable it may seem at the moment."

"Like what?"

"Well, for one thing, it looks bad. It's a shock. I spent a long time trying to figure out what it meant. Anybody from the church who saw you would wonder too. I worry they might not be able to handle it in a mature way. Might blow it way out of proportion."

"So, I've got enough problems as a pastor without making people wonder where I am and what I'm doing?"

"Something like that."

"Makes sense. I don't want to make ministry any more difficult than it already is."

"Yeah. There's another thing."

"Shoot."

"Aside from how it affects other people, being in a situation like that isn't good for you. Maybe I'm old-fashioned, but I don't think you ever want to walk into temptation open-eyed. At the bank, we've got security measures with the money. They don't prevent every scheme for stealing, but they keep us from being tempted. Two people handling money at all times. Cameras over the tellers. If you take away those things, you place the opportunity to steal a lot nearer to a person's impulses. No matter who you are, no matter how spiritual you may be, you can always be tempted. The thing that wasn't smart about what you did yesterday afternoon was placing an opportunity closer to your impulses."

"I willingly put myself in temptation."

"Right. It seems like sins are always calling, trying to lead a guy away from goodness. I don't want sin to succeed with you."

"So the real problem here is that I walked into a compromising situation with my eyes wide open."

"I think so."

"Not so much the appearances, though they're pretty bad."

"Right. The appearances are bad, but the situation is worse."

I could feel the back of my legs relax. I was getting the point across. We weren't getting bogged down trying to establish what had happened and why.

Dave was quiet for a moment, nodding his head. "I've got a real blind spot here. My generation doesn't think about these things. I mean, all the social structures that used to tell people what to do have broken down, and we're left to decide for ourselves how to act. There used to be—what's the word?— *decorum*. Back when marriages stayed together and women worked in the home, it was a lot clearer how a man should behave toward a woman who wasn't his wife. He didn't work with her at the office—at least not side-by-side. He didn't have a friendship with her. And he sure didn't ride around in a car with her. Things aren't clear now, with broken marriages and both sexes working together and ex-partners floating in and out of life. The decorum is gone."

While he was talking, it hit me that Dave was from a broken home. The Schmidts had gone to church, and both of Dave's parents had had born-again experiences. But I remembered their separation in the early eighties. Mrs. Schmidt felt unfulfilled in the marriage and was tired of what she thought was her husband's coldness. Or something like that. She wanted him to wake up, come alive, as she used to say. He never did—never became whatever it was she wanted. So they divorced.

She took little Dave. Left the church. Left town, even, for a few years. She brought Dave back in time for high school, and all of us watched him flounder.

When Dave was born again as a college student and went to seminary, it was like the all-things-work-together-for-good ending for everybody in the church who'd agonized and prayed over the Schmidt family. There were tears of joy on Dave's visits from school when he'd preach. People felt proud of his youth ministry at the church in the next town. When we had a vacancy, Dave appeared to be the obvious choice. It was God's will, it seemed. An answer to years of prayer.

Dave's blind spot, as he put it, made a lot of sense. Of course he wouldn't have known the decorum of past generations. How could he have learned it?

I'd been a jerk. "I hadn't thought about that side of things, Dave."

"No, don't take it that way. I'm not making excuses. Even if I have a blind spot, I'm still responsible to grow out of it and make some changes. What do you think I should do?"

I was getting further with Dave in this short conversation than I had in all the years before.

I shifted forward. "Well, let's talk about the message that clothing sends. A guy can dress on the older side of the spectrum or the younger. He can look like a grandpa or a teenager, and he can hit anywhere in between. The younger you dress, the more available you make yourself for the women. That's my opinion, anyway. Women signal availability by showing skin, men by showing youth. Maybe you could dress a little older. I don't mean light-blue polyester pants and plaid shirts. Just a little more formal. It would send a signal."

"Yeah, I can see that. It would definitely raise the decorum."

"Another thing: your manner, your way of relating with people. You could be a little more distant, especially with the younger women."

"Distant? What do you mean?"

"Well, you have a tendency to come alongside a person you're talking with. At least that's what I've seen. Wherever the person is, you have a sixth sense of how to get there yourself. With the old ladies, you're a grandson. With the old men, you're inquisitive, respectful. With the younger women, you're—"

"Flirtatious?"

"No, no, I don't mean that. No. More like . . . charming. A little too charming and warm. Smile less—smaller."

"Smile smaller?"

"Yeah. Put on a little authoritative ice. You don't have to be pompous or stuck-up. Just more reserved."

"I think I know what you mean. As a pastor, I'm not a young person's equal and I shouldn't try to act like it."

"Exactly."

We were both smiling. I'd expected resistance, I guess, and when Dave was so open, I thought the problem had disappeared. Though I knew no more about why Dave had been in that car than when I'd arrived, the fact that we understood each other made it seem not to matter. Still, for whatever reason—whether it sprang from some doubt or from impulse, I don't know—the question slipped out.

"Dave, who was that gal, anyway?"

5

"I went to high school with her. Her name is Kim."

Dave said this without any particular tone. He wasn't dismissing her as insignificant, but he wasn't giving any hint of whether she was important, either. Instead, the information was delivered like a news summary on the radio. Flat. They went to high school together. Her name was Kim.

I thought I noticed a slight change in his posture, too, though nothing I could put my finger on. It was like his whole body became an idling engine.

This was far from typical: Dave was either in gear or asleep. Most guys in meetings are inert as cinder blocks. Do they agree? Do they have a problem? Are they hostile, indifferent, or what? Dave, on the other hand, was easy to talk to. He seemed to track with you phrase by phrase—eyes widening, head nodding, torso leaning. So when he went blank for those few seconds, I thought it was strange.

Dave suddenly brightened. "You know, Jim, what you've been saying about decorum is very convicting. The more I think about Kim, I see meeting her was like a series of doors. I kept opening the next one.

"See, I'm always having little reunions with old high school acquaintances. We remember our teachers' crazy habits. We compete a little over who's climbed higher on the success ladder. And as we talk, they see that I'm different from what I was. They put that together with my unexpected career and they ask about the change. Then we talk about spiritual things.

"So when Kim walked into Basic Bean, it wasn't a complete surprise. I'd been wondering if I'd see her, whether she was still around. We saw each other out of the corners of our eyes, but we didn't try to connect. We sat in different places for about twenty minutes. Then she got up to throw a napkin away or something and moved in the direction of my table. We made eye contact and it was, 'Aren't you Dave?' and 'Aren't you Kim?' and we had the little reunion.

"Up to this point, I don't see any problem with the way I handled the situation. It's a common enough thing."

"Right. Happens all the time."

"So we started talking. It was the usual drill: Have you seen so-and-so? Do you remember Mr. Starkley sucking down cigarettes between classes? Where'd you go to grad school? But we're in this uncomfortable situation. I'm sitting down, she's standing up. It's obvious the conversation will go on for a while. Do I ask her to sit down?

"It seemed like the natural and polite thing to do, so I asked her. I was enjoying myself. In high school, Kim wasn't just a passing acquaintance or somebody from a different clique. This was a significant friendship and it would've been rude not to ask her to sit down for a minute. Actually, it never occurred to me not to ask . . . which is probably the sort of thing you're talking about, Jim."

Yes and no. I had talked about clear breaches of decorum—those unwise and unthinking steps toward privacy and unwarranted familiarity. What he was describing was a social courtesy in a public situation—asking an old friend to sit down for a bit after a chance meeting. But I could see where Dave was headed. All that kids of his generation saw in these situations was a series of grays—if they even saw that. Maybe they didn't see a series. Maybe all situations washed together. Asking the woman to sit down and getting into her car may have been indistinguishable. And that point was relevant.

"Yeah, Dave, I guess that is the sort of thing. That's the sort of situation where we can start compromising. I don't necessarily think you did compromise anything there. It was still a public situation. But, you're right, that was the place to be watchful."

"Well, I think it gets worse. We talked quite a while and eventually she squinted at me. 'I can't believe you used to be this party animal and now you're a preacher.'

"So I gave her my testimony, how far down I went in college and how much healthier I was after I came to Christ. Her eyes never left my face.

"By the time I finished, she had leaned toward me. 'So are you happy being a pastor?'

"I smiled. 'Most of the time, yeah. There are hard times, but I learn from them.'

"She cocked her head. 'What are the hard times?'

"'When I'm misunderstood or rejected. People sometimes leave the church, no matter how much I've invested in them. All sorts of crisis situations can pile up—unemployment, illness, death. Takes a lot out of me.'

"She raised her eyebrows. 'Didn't think about those things. I guess you're the man everyone runs to.' She pulled back. 'I couldn't do that. I never know what to tell people when they have real problems.'

"'I'm no different. I rarely know what to tell them, and all the intense conversations leave me feeling empty. But I do get to see Jesus do his thing.'

"She was so open. I found myself talking about all sorts of things I don't normally get into, like my family. I didn't question it until now. I wonder whether I inadvertently crossed another boundary, sharing those kinds of personal things. Maybe we slipped back into the way we used to talk. Who knows? Anyway, I think it was a breach, and I missed it completely at the time."

I compressed my lips. "That's a good call, Dave."

"Well, there was one other step—obviously. I mean, I got in her car." Dave paused. "I'm just being straight, Jim. It's hard, but I want to be accountable."

He sighed lightly. "After we shared for a while, she said, 'I'd love to see your church.' I should've invited her to come on Sunday, told her where it was, service times, and all that. But that wasn't what she wanted. She wanted me to show her what my life meant now, what the place signified. It was like, 'You've changed and I want to see how important that change is.' She was making a claim on our past friendship, if that makes any sense.

"I had more work to do, and I'd planned to stay longer at the Bean. She had to go. To me, it didn't make sense to meet her at the church—go in separate cars. I didn't even consider it. I just said, 'The church is close by. Let's take your car over, look around, and then you can drop me back here.'

"So we did. I left my books and we drove off. And you know what the scary thing is, Jim? I see now that I really wanted that time with her."

6

Twenty-four hours later, when I drove to the meeting of the trustees that I'd called, I understood why Dave had made all those confessions. By that time, it was easy to explain his freewill offerings of culpability—explain them strategically. A few minutes of sorting and labeling would've been sufficient, if I'd had the stomach for it.

But at the time Dave made those confessions, such explanations were impossible because they were unnecessary. There was no apparent strategy to explain. All of his words and expressions, even his motivations, had a restful logic in the immediate context. And it didn't even occur to me that he and I might be talking about a different gospel.

For me, this was a moment to redeem the church's history of anger. Our pastors had been punished for every failing, every misunderstanding, every stray word and irritable tone. They had been punished for acting and not acting; speaking and not speaking; punished when they came, and punished when they went.

Dad had inflicted a large share of that punishment. His advice was almost always good, but his anger made it seem worthless. If he had stopped the recriminations and the prideful lectures, some of his wisdom and expertise might have nourished people. But his wisdom was poisoned by his ungraciousness.

Now I could do it differently. I could call a pastor to account and be gracious at the same time. This was an opportunity for me to set aside the worst things about Dad and salvage the best.

By the end of Dave's confessions, I was determined to comfort him. I thought he was being too hard on himself.

"Maybe you did want to go with her, Dave. I'm sure you had all kinds of nostalgic memories while you were talking with her. There's nothing wrong with that. It's not a sin to be pleased with the way your life has turned out, or to want to share it with an old friend. Your desires aren't the issue. This is about decorum. I'm not here to say your heart is bad."

"I appreciate that, Jim. But I do think my desires played a role here."

"Maybe. Maybe you did want to get in that car. But is it a sin to want something like that? The issue is what you do, not what you want. Just be smarter next time. Be able to find your way with more discretion. I don't want to get into murky stuff like what you desired or didn't desire.

"Look, you know as well as I do that sin is like filth; if you want to be clean, you stay away from it. When you get some filth on you, you wash it off. That's what Jesus is all about, right? He cleans you up from whatever muck you've blundered into. The point is, put some space between you and sin. Don't get into abstract things you can't settle, like desires and motivations. You'll only beat yourself up."

Dave looked at the floor. "I'm supposed to be a minister of the gospel to you, and here you are ministering to me."

I couldn't say anything for a while. After an uncomfortable silence, I took a deep breath. "I guess I have to make amends."

Dave looked up. "Make amends? For what?"

"For all the mean-spirited people who led this church for years. For Dad."

"Your dad wasn't mean."

"Yes he was. Very few people would be capable of that *Accounting-for-Dummies* crack. Especially when you'd paid more attention to his advice than any pastor in years."

Dave adjusted one of the pieces on the game board. Then he shrugged. "Your dad had some issues. He needed to admit it. But he had a lot of wisdom, too. You have to pay attention to the wisdom, not just the weakness."

"You impacted his life with that approach. If he'd lived, he would've softened."

"He *was* softening. Remember, the *Accounting-for-Dummies* moment was five years ago. He never said anything like that again, in public or private."

"Yeah, but did he ever apologize?"

"No. I never expected him to apologize."

"He should've."

Dave smiled. "Why? What he said wasn't wrong, just hurtful. We all say hurtful things. When someone stops being hurtful, I take the change as apology enough."

"I could use a little of that attitude."

"I think you've already got it, Jim. You shouldn't feel you have to make amends for everybody in the past, least of all your dad. You held me accountable today, but you did it because you care about me."

"That's what the body of Christ is for. Accountability and grace."

Dave smiled again. "Thanks for coming by, Jim."

"No problem. Maybe we should pray before I go."

"I'd really appreciate that."

At that point, I found myself in the middle of an old problem.

We're commanded to pray. So we pray over our food. We pray over our meetings. We hold meetings for the express purpose of praying. Prayer ought to be one of the most important things we do.

But if prayer was supposed to be the center of my relationship with God, then I didn't have much of a relationship. I certainly felt that God was important. I tried to maintain my relationship with him. But I thought the best way to do that was to obey him. If he says, "Don't do this," then don't. If he says, "Do this," then do. I was frankly suspicious of people who prayed too long. I often knew they weren't obeying God in one area or another, and a lot of the time they were caked with the mud of unconfessed sin. I had a suspicion that their prayers were a cover-up—or at best a makeup assignment—for not obeying.

Like Dad. He could come home from a church meeting where he'd just savaged the pastor and the board and then pray the longest suppertime prayer you ever heard. He'd make his way down the list of relations, and by the time he got to our cousins, my brother and I'd be wondering how cold the tuna casserole was going to be. The sudden piety offended me.

If I was supposed to obey God—and if that was what I needed to focus on—then why pray? Shouldn't I zero in on my responsibilities instead of reminding God of his? Sure, there were times when events had gotten out of my control, when I couldn't do the essential things. When Audrey got cancer, that's when I prayed. I had to pray then because I couldn't do anything else. But when there were things I could do, like obey God, I never understood why I should waste time praying—if I can say it that way.

So here Dave and I were. We'd settled the matter. His responsibilities were clear, or so it seemed to me. He had accepted my counsel, taken the lessons to heart, and was applying them. He was even getting overzealous. Yet I had suggested prayer. I'd had nothing particular in mind to pray for, but it had seemed like the right way to wrap things up.

What would I say? It was time for the formulas: thank first, ask second. Maybe while I was thanking I'd be able to remember something to ask for.

Before the silence could stretch to awkwardness, I dove in. "Thank you, Lord, for this time we've shared, this time of open conversation. Thanks for the relationship Dave and I have, our camaraderie and brotherliness. Our friendship. I just thank you for Dave's openness and his willingness to learn. And his honesty." Aha! "I pray that you'd give me the same spirit, the same ability to be teachable. I want that openness to correction for myself, Lord." Now some kind of send-off. "Go with us this evening, Lord, and help us to obey you. In Jesus' name, amen."

We lifted our faces and enjoyed a pleased but uncertain stillness, of the sort that often follows a prayer. I had a habit of using this time to think of a joke. It seemed to me that because things tended to get heavy and ponderous before prayers, it made sense to lighten them up afterward. Especially in cases like this.

I leaned forward in my seat, as if ready to leave, and smiled real big. "Hey, yesterday was only Tuesday. What were you doing all dressed up? Khakis and your sport coat and everything!"

I wish I could put into words what I saw in Dave's face and body language, for a split second. Whereas before he had slipped into neutral, this time it was like he left and returned without his body going anywhere. I didn't merely see a lack of expression; I saw vacancy for an instant—the drive-through window open, but no one inside to take my order.

All of a sudden, he was back—his presence reasserted in his pupils. He laughed, but it was one of those forced chuckles betrayed by an unnatural rhythm. He adjusted more pieces on the game board. "Dressed up? No reason."

Men are famous for their delayed comprehension. The weird relational atmosphere I'd smelled hadn't yet been absorbed through the lining of my lungs into my bloodstream. So I pressed my little joke. "Aw, come on. It takes a funeral or some-thing shattering like that to get you into tailored clothing during the week."

"I guess I thought a funeral had been scheduled." This was meant to be a lighthearted comeback, but it had an edge.

It's a real problem to recover from a tease that has come across badly. This one had exposed a nerve, insensitively bringing back a previous issue. Should I persist in that line of joshing, playing dumb and hoping it dawned on Dave that I didn't mean anything by it? Should I drop it and reassure him that I was kidding—an admission of incompetence? Or should I admit I'd messed up royally by injecting my actual feelings into the remark, and then mount a full-scale retreat—apologies, the works?

Think fast. Middle course. "I'm just kidding, Dave."

"I guess the T-shirts are too far toward the young end of the spectrum. Maybe a little unprofessional."

Yikes. "It's just not every day you dress up. That's all."

"No, you're right. We talked about this. I need to look more like a pastor. It's safer that way."

"Well, yes, but I didn't mean to make a rude crack about it."

"No, no. Don't worry about it."

Apology not quite offered. Apology not quite accepted. It would have to do.

I tried to steer out of the embarrassment. "Seriously, was there a funeral yesterday? Did I miss something?"

Now Dave sighed heavily. "There wasn't a funeral. I dressed up for a totally different reason. I guess this problem with Kim goes deeper than decorum. I'm starting to realize that I have some issues that need to be resolved."

I eased back into my seat.

"See, I had noticed Kim at Basic Bean before this. Usually in line, ordering something to go. There's always a rush between 3:00 and 3:30—people sent to get mochas for the office, that sort of thing. She'd be one of those, and there'd always be such a mob that she wouldn't stop to look around. So she never noticed me sitting there—or she never recognized me.

"She's pretty attractive, I'll admit. More so than when we were teenagers. Actually, much more so. I was curious about the change in her, just like she became curious about me. I wanted to meet her again, Jim. This wasn't the accident I made it out to be. I was subtly trying to be more visible. That's what I meant when I talked about wanting to drive off with her. It wasn't about displaying my new life. It was about her. I dressed up to get her attention."

He was infatuated with the woman.

My mental digestion wasn't at maximum efficiency by this time. I was tired. I wanted to go home. So the size of this admission impressed itself on me only gradually.

"The truth is, I think there are reasons why I'm open to this kind of encounter. I'm having trouble with Amy. I'm frustrated. Here we've been married all these years and we have these great kids, but I'm—I just have to be blunt with you, Jim—I'm unhappy. There's no pleasure in this marriage anymore. It's not that I don't love her. Not at all. But we seem to be in an unrewarding period right now. I know I have to take some steps to get us out of it, but I can't work up the will. I don't have any motivation."

He was infatuated with the woman. He called her attractive. He wanted to meet her. He dressed up on a Tuesday to get her attention. It was deliberate.

"I'm actually an orderly person, Jim. It may not appear that way, what with my clothes and all, but I am. For one thing, I like a solid routine. I don't just like it, I have to have one or I don't function well. I make each day the same: breakfast at 6:30; office at 8:30 for busywork and phone calls; Basic Bean after lunch for study and appointments. If one day isn't the same as the others, I get irritable. Another thing: I like stuff kept neat. I like the house clean, tidy. Pencils where the pencils go, dishes where the dishes go, shoes in the closet, toys picked up. Things out of place drive me crazy.

"Amy is not an orderly person. She doesn't have a schedule. She sleeps late, doesn't get the kids up till the last minute, doesn't have a plan for the day. I have a hard time respecting her. Well, I don't respect her. She's too spontaneous. She'll show up at people's houses without even calling to see whether they're home. She'll suddenly pile everybody in the car and go off to a restaurant or a movie, which we can't afford. She says it'll be fun, but it never is because she doesn't think ahead. It's too late to go to that restaurant, because you always have a forty-five minute wait after 5:30. Things like that. She messes up my plans."

My pastor was infatuated with another woman.

He had seen her day after day for who knows how long. He'd watched her standing in line, giving her order, putting cream in her coffee. He had become interested, and then attracted, and then infatuated. He had let this happen to himself.

"Another thing is, she won't discuss issues with me. I'm interested in some of the deeper things of life—philosophy and psychology, and culture, that kind of thing. She isn't. She couldn't care less about what motivates us to do things, or why God put certain passages in the Bible, or what we can do to reach the seekers in our society. When I try to discuss these things with her, it's like she rejects me. She clams up and acts like these big issues aren't worth her time—or mine. All she wants to talk about is the kids and the next family day trip. It's like her horizon isn't any broader than that. There's a whole world of issues out there, but I can't share those things with her."

"You're infatuated with the woman."

"With Amy?"

"With Kim."

"I don't follow you."

It took some time for me to get all of this straight. Dave had to explain his marital problems twice over again, and as he did, the picture grew sharper in my mind: his desires really were the issue. The problem was not external things that intruded on his life to tempt him. The problem was that he sought temptation and deliberately exposed himself to an opportunity.

His breach of decorum with Kim had been driven by internal things.

After imagining I'd solved all these simple problems, that I'd dispelled the mystery around Dave's failings, I now saw that the problems were neither solved nor simple, and his failings were more mysterious than ever. We had slid from a discussion about immaturity to one about infatuation. What had been on the dry land of actions was now sunk in the bog of desires. We were moving backward, it seemed to me at the time.

And what was worse, I didn't have any way of talking about desires like these. I had said desires weren't sins. But I hadn't been thinking of this kind. Suddenly I was counseling a kid, a delayed adolescent shattered by discovering that his wife was a person, not a fantasy. A kid infatuated with another fantasy.

What were Dave's desires—understandable but mistaken, understandable but unhealthy, or just plain wrong? Would I tell Dave his desires had to change? How would I tell him that? And how would I advise him to go about changing them?

There was a quick knock at the door and Amy peeked in.

7

"You guys want some dinner?"

Dave let all the tension built up in his shoulders go slack. "Yeah, honey, that'd be great."

Amy remained in the hallway, looking into the office from behind the door, with one hand curled around the edge. Her face suspended there, she looked at us with mock rebuke. The rebuke was somewhere in her eyebrows, undermined by a slight tug at the sides of her mouth. She was as gentle and quiet a woman as I could imagine, yet her face could tease you relentlessly.

Men fall in one of two camps on the matter of other men's wives. Either they can't understand why a man isn't more in love with his wife, or they can't fathom what attracted him to her in the first place.

Men often believe their friends and coworkers are married to ridiculous women—women who don't have any sense or charm, but who act as if they have both. We realize this at social gatherings where people talk too much. We sit and listen to these wives tell stories about their husbands' physical ailments, as if they were doing a stand-up routine to an audience not yet silly drunk. We listen to their narrow but confidently delivered opinions about the lack of security at public schools. We endure the piercing shrieks of their laughter, and we wonder (even discussing it later) what could've sparked the romance between these women and our otherwise competent, rational friends.

But just as often, we see men married to wonderful women—women who are physically winsome and who also have well-proportioned, shapely minds—men joined to a kind of greatness, but who waste no opportunity to express their contempt for her. A woman can know a lot, talk well, and even banter easily, while her husband sits off to the side shaking his head. We discuss this pettiness as often as we discuss the other mysteries of male-female relationships, and we occasionally agonize over it.

Dave had said that he didn't respect his wife. *He must be nuts.* How could he not respect the irony in that face peering around the door? How could he not respect the service Amy gave, the selflessness? Why did he feel that his inner life had to be defended against this woman?

Amy looked at the table where we sat. "Shall I bring it in here so you can keep talking?"

Before Dave could respond, I butted in, "Thanks, Amy, but I really need to get going. I just have a couple of things I need to nail down with your husband, and then I'll let him go. Ten minutes. I promise."

Mock skepticism. She withdrew and eased the door shut—keeping the knob turned so the door wouldn't latch with a loud click.

Now, somehow, we were going to deal with Dave's attitude. We would deal with it graciously, and we'd do so in ten minutes, but we were still going to deal with it.

I spoke low. "Dave, what's the bottom line? Are you going to let your marriage go this way—go cold? Or are you going to do something about it?"

"It's already gone cold. That's what I'm trying to tell you, Jim. This marriage can't get any colder. It can only get angrier—and I'm afraid it's going to."

"You talk about your marriage like it's an ocean current, like you're drifting on it and dreading the direction it's taking. Marriage isn't that way." I turned my palms up. "I'm no psychologist, but I have been married twenty-six years, and I know that marriages don't just happen. Good or bad, they're made. You're making your marriage right now, and you've been making it all this time."

That was tougher than I'd intended, but it was true.

A man makes his wife who she is, whether he likes it or not. He makes vows to a flawed woman—a woman he ought to know is flawed from the start—and the way he treats her either amplifies the flaws or the strengths. A man has to find his wife's strengths, dispel the mystery around her flaws, and help her succeed.

I knew it was true because I'd lived it.

I had been through the honeymoon, with all its joys and disappointments. I had felt the satisfaction of feeling settled, of being able to sleep well at night for the first time. But I'd also felt the disappointments of the wedding night, the realization that what I'd anticipated as a religious experience was another kind of normal living. You spend your teens imagining it, and instead of the room being transformed into a temple, it remains a hotel.

I'd been through the same tough period as Dave, when the joys became memories while the disappointments took on a life of their own.

I'd seen Audrey's tendency to withdraw, for instance, when we were still dating. I'd gone to her apartment one night after work and she wouldn't talk—not about her day, not about my day, not about where to go for dinner, nothing. But the next evening, she was back to her old chatty, teasing, curious self.

Audrey was flawed, and I knew it.

But I didn't give it much thought. So the longer we were married, the more I saw this flaw and the more I resented it. She swallowed one issue after another, digesting them inside herself behind a pretty smile. She talked with her friends instead of with me. There was little left for us to discuss but who, what, when, and where. *Why* was verboten. Her withdrawals became living inhabitants in our home—unwelcome guests—while our former ways of talking became distant relations that we sent anniversary cards to.

What I didn't realize until years later was that I had made this wife—I had turned her flaw into a pattern. Early on, I showed her my own flaws, and she figured out how she would handle me. Whenever she described her real problems and feelings, I was dismissive. I bellowed at her, acting like the answers to her questions were so obvious that they weren't even worth talking about. I wasn't doing it consciously. My mistreatment of her had the sincerity of thoughtlessness. But my disregard set her policy in concrete; my callousness only stiffened her resolve.

Classic.

I found out what was going on through sheer persistence—clumsy, unfocused, reactive masculine prying. I calculated that a sharp but temporary stab of humiliation would be better than the dull but permanent bruise of loneliness. I decided to push her with questions until I found out why she wouldn't talk to me. What's the matter? Why don't we talk anymore? What do your friends have that I don't? Over a period of weeks, I drove her to the extremity of telling me the truth. And the truth was that I had begun to create my marriage even before the wedding.

Through the grapevine, Audrey had discovered that her best friend and future maid-of-honor didn't like me. In fact, her friend thought I was boring while pretending to Audrey's face that I was the greatest thing that'd ever happened to her. Audrey tried to tell me how badly this hurt her. She got through about three sentences before I said, "Oh, that doesn't matter!" and smiled as if it were no big deal that her closest friend had been two-faced and catty.

That wasn't what humiliated me. I didn't even remember the incident. I still don't. What humiliated me was realizing that if it had happened that very day, I would've had the same reaction. After six years of marriage, I hadn't learned any more about her needs than I'd known when we were engaged. Why would she confide in someone who didn't give her feelings a second thought?

In my mind's eye, my mom started wincing and giving me the round-eye treatment. She had still been alive back then and had surely seen my neglect, but she never said anything.

Just seeing the truth about myself hadn't been enough. I still had to do something about it. I had made one wife, and now I had to make a different one from the same woman. I had to figure out, by trial and error, which of my attitudes and habits had pushed her away, and I had to replace them. I had to hope that her love for me had remained strong enough for her to see my changes and trust me more.

I made transforming my marriage my life's work, a business to become expert in. And I succeeded.

For five years I trained myself in being quick to listen and slow to speak. At first, I tried biting my tongue, but I ended up cutting it out altogether. I tried giving better advice, but eventually gave none. I tried using body language to show I was listening. Later, I just tried to listen. I made mental recordings of our conversations and played them back, doing performance reviews based on all the how-to-communicate-with-your-spouse books I left lying on my nightstand—such are the male's resources in sending subtle messages. I took Audrey on weekend trips to her favorite places, trying to implement the recommendations from a half-dozen troubled-marriage manuals.

The sum of it all made the difference.

I say "the sum" because the training disciplines themselves accomplished little or nothing, but the dogged, tireless energy I put into them showed Audrey that I was determined to learn even in the face of comprehensive failure. She took my determination for love. Whether she was motivated by pity or amusement, I don't know, but she started to talk to me again. And this time she found a willing, even obsessive listener.

So in my conversation with Dave, I felt we'd finally landed on something I could talk about with some authority. And at this point, he got his back up.

"Are you blaming me for my wife's disorganization?"

"Yes."

"You're saying that I drove her away so she won't talk to me?"

"You got it."

"That's crazy, Jim. She was that way before we were married. She was disorganized and unresponsive. She could never keep her classwork straight, never had any structure for accomplishing anything, was on time only by accident. And she never seemed interested in what I wanted to talk about. I didn't make her that way."

"So you saw these things before you were married."

"Sure I did."

"What'd you marry her for, then?"

"I didn't know they'd bother me this much!"

"In other words, her flaws and frailties are not your problem? They aren't responsibilities you took on when you married her? They're like the flaws in a car or a house—things you put up with until you can't stand it anymore? And then you trade her in on a newer model?"

"I don't want to 'trade her in,' but I can't make her change."

"Not with that point of view, you can't."

"So you're actually saying that it's my responsibility to make my wife change."

I paused, but I was nodding my head. "I'll admit you can't force her to change. I'm not talking about coercion. But you have to realize she's always responding to who you are. Not what you *do*—who you *are*. And if you want her to be different, if you want any chance to improve your marriage at all, you'll have to figure out how your character has influenced her, and you'll have to change. Her response is not guaranteed. But *your* changing is the way *her* changing becomes possible. Every man makes his wife."

Dave's lip froze into a curl. "There's not a single Christian psychologist anywhere who'd agree with you."

"I don't care."

"But aren't people responsible for their own actions? Don't they have to decide on their own that they need to change?"

"Yes. But what brings people to that point?"

Dave leaned forward. "An extreme problem. When they feel too much pressure, they decide they need to change."

"You and I both know that's not true, Dave. How much pressure has Marty Worthington created for himself for how many years? His drinking debilitates him more and more, he's alienated more business associates than I've ever had, and even his talents are deteriorating. His financial picture has never been worse, to the point that he'd probably never dig out of his debts if he became a model businessman tomorrow. He took one of the prettiest women in town and made her a physical wreck by giving her more anxiety than anyone should have to bear. And his sons won't talk to him, except to tell him what a louse he is to their mother. It doesn't matter how much pressure he's under. He comes to church more regularly when it gets rough. He goes for counseling when things get really tight. But he doesn't change even the smallest of his bad habits. It never ceases to amaze me how much pressure people can handle."

"So, answer your own question, Jim. What makes someone decide to change?"

"Hope."

Dave said nothing. I would've thought that a pastor, of all people, would understand how hope softens us. But Dave just stared at the game board.

"Amy is a phenomenal woman, Dave. She has so many strengths, not the least of which is compassion. Don't you think if you offered her some hope, all her goodness would stir?"

"I'm the one who needs hope. Why can't she give me some hope?"

"Because it doesn't work that way."

"What do you mean?"

"Wives can't change their husbands. They all try, and they all fail. Husbands change their wives. She's never going to give you hope until you give some to her. Your hope comes from the hope you foster in her by changing your own character."

"I didn't realize you were so sexist."

"Make fun if you want. But I'm talking reality, not ideology."

"Do you have any basis for all this? Is there a book on this?"

"The only one I've found is the book of Ephesians: 'Husbands, love your wives, even as Christ also loved the church, and gave himself for it.'"

Dave stared intently at the game board. After a while, he looked me right in the eye. "Based on what I've described, why do you think Amy's not interested in talking about anything?"

"You said it yourself—you don't respect her. Would you want to have a deep discussion with a person who doesn't respect you? Do you think she can live with you and not know your attitude?"

Dave looked back at the game. "You're saying that I can give her hope by gaining respect for her."

"Right."

"Which means the respect has to be real. We're not just talking about positive words every now and then."

"Right."

"What do I do with her disorganization? How do I respect her when she brings chaos into my life? Just ignore it?"

"Give her a goal. A small one, maybe, but one she can definitely meet. Then give her another one. Show her over time how you want things to go."

"That sounds like an employer, not a husband. I can't give her orders like that."

"Well, no, you don't leave a memo in the kitchen. You bring it up like, 'I really need some things to be different when I get home,' or whatever. 'Can we start with this?' And then you negotiate it. But the key is you have to focus on the immediate improvement and ignore the other irritants. You have to teach her and teach yourself at the same time."

Dave glanced at the game board again and then gave me a weary look. "Will you help me do this, Jim? I want to do it. Will you help?"

8

It had been a close one. I'd almost lost him. When you're that tough on a guy, you're making a bet that something inside will keep him from blowing you off. And it's usually a poor bet.

Dave easily could have said, "You don't know what you're talking about! You don't know my needs! No one understands me at this church! I quit!" There are few limits on people's options anymore; they can move away from a whole set of relationships and start a new life in another suburb exactly like this one, and they can get another credit card to pay for it. The gravity of influence that once held people in orbit is gone.

Dave's spiritual office only increased the likelihood that he'd blow me off. It's not exactly a minor revelation when the pastor says he's unhappy in his marriage. He's vulnerable, so there's pressure on you to be levelheaded. Plus, you're supposed to be respectful in any advice you give. My getting tough on him broke a lot of rules and gave him a ready excuse to pull rank. His pride was at stake, not just his autonomy.

Worse, I had withheld the incentives to cooperate that people expect when they make confessions like his. Dave might've expected leniency from me, but I didn't give him any—at least not on the point of his unhappiness. He was going to have to face the consequences of his marital neglect. He also might have expected some empathy, but I denied him that, too. Maybe most important of all, I had withheld the reasonable tone that enables men to make concessions in tense moments without losing face. I had allowed no pretense that we were both making compromises.

On what did I base my bet?

Hope. Somewhere in his soul, Dave had to have some dusting of hope that he could still make a fulfilling marriage with Amy. Had to. It was inevitable. As certain as the four seasons. All men have this hope. I just had to speak to it—maybe bellow at it a little—and it would assert itself. I just needed to supply a place for the hope to stand.

So when Dave asked for help, I thought I had won my bet, and I cashed in. Sure I'd help. Be glad to. It'd be a privilege to help a man prove his hope. And my win felt huge because I'd placed everything on it, all the ambition I'd nurtured for years to do church graciously. The fulfillment of my desire to show how forgiveness could prevail had been at risk during a few minutes of toughness, and the risk had been worth it.

Later, I almost admired how Dave outmaneuvered me so simply. At the time, I didn't consider myself gullible. In fact, I harbored a self-image of worldliness. Though I was one of the good guys, I felt I understood how the bad guys worked. I even imagined I might've made just as cunning a bad guy as the rest. More cunning. This confidence that I'd be able to spot a lie was my downfall. The lying that evening was beyond anything I'd ever dreamed.

By the time I drove to the trustee meeting on Thursday night, my sense of triumph would be gone. The A-frame outlines of our 1960s-era church building would no longer look like an inspiring house founded on the bedrock of love and justice. It would look more like a Bedouin tent pitched in sand, blasted by heat and stiffened by cold, stretched and sagging from too much tearing down and setting up. When I saw it, I would remember my elation the previous evening and I would be nauseated. I would wonder whether Moses had ever regretted talking God out of his wrath on Mount Sinai.

But my delight at vindication still had a half-hour to live when I left Dave's house.

I arrived home faint with hunger. Audrey was doing a crossword puzzle at the kitchen table and didn't look up. "A bunch of Rachel's friends came by and ate all your dinner. Nothing left but asparagus. I tried to stop them."

"Sorry I'm late."

"You're forgiven. But you're still going to starve."

I opened the fridge. On the middle shelf was a plate with generous portions of Swiss steak, potatoes, and beans covered in plastic wrap. "There's food in here."

"Oh! They must've heeded my pleas after all."

I confronted the microwave, holding the plate and staring at the control panel.

Audrey still didn't look up. "Bottom right."

I pushed a lever and the door opened.

"Power."

More staring. You'd think it would be obvious, but the keypad on the new microwave looked like it had one of those Hewlitt-Packard engineering calculators built in. And all I wanted to do was heat up my dinner.

"Power—top row of buttons, second from the left."

Beep.

"Time. Second row of buttons."

Beep.

"Try two minutes. That's a *two* followed by two zeros . . . where all the numbers are."

I scowled at her. "I'm not helpless."

When the final beep sounded, I took my steaming plate to the table and settled into a chair across from Audrey.

She continued her crossword in silence, and I left her on tenterhooks. Eventually she set it down. "Am I going to have to go to the stables and get the wild horses? What kept you so late?"

"Wild horses don't live in stables."

"Talk!"

"It's a long story, but satisfying." I told Audrey how I'd seen Dave get out of Kim's Mercedes. ("Mercedes?!") I summarized my conversation at Dave's house, how the matter seemed at first to be about decorum but quickly grew larger. ("Decorum?!") My thrill at breaking the spiritual bank was already ebbing.

"Well, just wait. It gets better." I told about Dave's unhappiness with Amy. ("This is better?") I also told what my response had been: learn to be a husband. ("That's better.") Then I leaned in. I gave a blow-by-blow of Dave's resistance, trying to intensify the drama of his plea for help. But all I did was drain the last few drips of my enthusiasm. "See, honey? He really wants my help!" I laughed.

Audrey was looking at me with a combination of . . . well, I don't know what it was a combination of, but it was clear she wasn't onboard with my story.

After a moment, her jaw muscles snapped back into gear. "So our pastor's unhappy in his marriage and becomes infatuated with this . . . Kim. He seizes a little privacy with her in her Mercedes. And they begin what sounds like some pretty serious flirting. Or have I missed something?"

"No, you've summarized it quite nicely, dear."

"But you're sure he'll be a better husband once you've counseled him?"

I slapped the fork down. "Cut me a little slack here! I've been trying to figure out what to do for two days! Do I know how to handle pastors who are disappointed in their marriages? No. Did they train me in psychology for my MBA? No. You think I don't know how bad this is? You haven't had to live with my stomach today. Believe me, I know how bad it is. I'm just a simple guy trying to figure out what to do with his teenage pastor."

"I'm sorry, Jim. I didn't—"

"Something half this bad could split the church. And I'm the one who has to run the meetings. I know how bad this is."

"Jim, I'm sorry."

I rammed some beans into my mouth, hoping they would keep it busy.

Audrey patted the table with her fingertips. "This is just a little shocking. I didn't mean to attack you."

"It's okay."

We looked at opposite sides of the kitchen in silence.

I sighed. "I just want to do this right, Audrey. Every time the church has a crisis, it starts throwing people away. No forgiveness, no patience. Running Dave out would be easy. But helping him overcome his failings is the right thing to do."

Audrey looked at me and pursed her lips. "Yes. But some failings are harder to forgive than others. Dave and Amy didn't take their vacation together last April, and now I know why. He doesn't want to be around her. I can't be neutral about behavior like that."

She was right; the incident with Kim seemed to be part of a pattern. Mom's wince was back in my mind's eye. I needed to do something—something more than offer help. This was not just a matter of renewing a man's hope.

But then Audrey pushed the problem to another level of difficulty. "Do you think he told you the truth?"

"What do you mean?"

"Well, Dave could've made this story up. I mean, what if he just invented the conversation with Kim to make the relationship seem innocent?"

When you're pondering a question like that, a bite of Swiss steak can last an awfully long time. I ground away at the implications of my pastor committing adultery and lying about it to my face. "Audrey, if he's discovered in a lie, it'll be horrible. He'll be humiliated. He'll scar his children, and lose Amy—he'll lose her even if she doesn't leave him. And he'll have to live with the guilt of what he's done for the rest of his life. I just can't picture Dave doing that much harm."

"Well, neither can I. I'm just saying . . ."

I was silent for a while, working a bit of Swiss steak out from between two teeth with my tongue. Then I started thinking out loud. "What would happen to the church if Dave were discovered in adultery? A split is just the beginning. Instead of two full services, we could end up with a single half-empty one. Giving could tank. Instead of children in the Sunday school rooms, we might hear crickets."

"I don't care about any of that," Audrey said. "I care what everyone will think if they find out you knew all these things but didn't pursue them? I can just hear the meeting: 'So, Jim, you're telling us he confessed to disrespecting his wife, becoming infatuated with another woman, and taking a little drive, all dressed up, in her Mercedes—confided it all to you right there in his home—but you didn't have the imagination to ask whether he'd actually had sex with the woman?' I don't want to sit through that."

"You're right. Dave could've lied." I chewed in silence for another minute or two. "But it seems impossible. He volunteered everything. I never had to drag an admission out of him, even when he was arguing with me at the end."

"He volunteered everything?"

"That's what was weird. Dave was the one who brought up Kim, not me. He said, 'Are you here about the gal who dropped me off yesterday?' If he had wanted to cover up adultery, surely he wouldn't have made the first move like that. He would've waited to hear what I asked and how. Then he could've decided how much to lie. That's elementary: you don't lie more than you have to."

"That's true."

"And the more we talked about decorum, the more openly he described his lapses."

"Openly?"

"Yeah. He told me how each step was taken toward the car ride. Each step. He understood exactly how wrong he'd been. If he were trying to hide adultery, why would he lead me down the trail he took toward it?"

"That's true, too." Audrey's face was expressionless.

"Dave was even the one to bring up his desires. He didn't pretend he was innocently drawn along. He outright told me that he wanted to be alone with her. And when I misunderstood, he went back to the issue and insisted on it. If he were trying to keep me from discovering adultery, or even asking about it, why would he admit what he could've falsified?"

. "Good question."

"He went further than that. He gave more detail than I wanted about his dissatisfaction with Amy. He practically invited me to speculate. A man who's trying to hide an affair doesn't reveal so much. He doesn't tell even the smallest part of what he's done if he doesn't have to. The risk of exposure is too great."

Still no expression. "Yeah, you're right. I can't argue with any of that." But then her eyebrows shot up. "What if he had another plan?"

"Another plan?"

"Yeah. He could've been more shrewd about it, could've tried to fake you out. Suppose he was trying to appear forthcoming and honest. Suppose he told one secret after another to make it seem silly for you to ask any more questions. Every one of his revelations would dampen your suspicion, keep you from wondering what other sins he might have hidden."

"I think I need to watch you more carefully."

"I'm serious!"

I chewed some more Swiss steak. "Well, it's possible. He could've done what you're saying. But think about how he'd have to plan it. To use a strategy like that, Dave would have to predict my responses to each of his disclosures—how I'd react when he told me about his infatuation with Kim, for example, or his dissatisfaction with Amy. And he'd have to know that his disclosures wouldn't make my curiosity worse."

"Maybe *I* ought to watch *you*."

"Well, think about it. Dave would have to predict that I'd interpret his getting in the car as naïve, or maybe the result of immaturity, not deliberate. He could only tell me he desired the car ride with Kim if he knew I'd call it infatuation, not lust. If he thought there was even a chance I'd jump to the ugliest conclusion with any of his confessions, his strategy would fail."

"But those were exactly your responses."

"Yes, but I don't see how he could've known them in advance. How could he have been that certain?"

"I don't know."

"Well, how about this? Dave would have to know that none of his disclosures would result in his being humiliated or fired. So he'd have to know my response would be to teach him, no matter how shocked I might be—that I'd respond with counsel instead of questioning his fitness to be our pastor."

"There again, that's exactly how you responded."

"Yeah, but could he have known that in advance?"

"Maybe."

"Oh, he might've *thought* I would respond that way. But I doubt he could've been certain enough to base his whole strategy on it."

Audrey didn't say anything.

"But the most crucial thing he'd have to know was that I'd be morally incapable of chasing him all the way to the truth."

"What?"

"He could only use your strategy if he was certain I had some guilt or complacency that would make me unable to hunt down the truth about his adultery."

"Even if you imagined the truth, you wouldn't be able to go after it?"

"Right. After all, there were no guarantees that I'd interpret his behavior charitably. So if those safeguards failed, he'd have to gamble that I would not pursue him because of some inner conflict of my own—maybe a sense of hypocrisy, or an idea that adultery was excusable in his case, or even simple cowardice."

"Well, you don't have any of those conflicts."

"No, I don't. Besides, he told me himself at the very beginning of the conversation—before he'd made any disclosures at all—that I was the sort of man who'd always do the right thing. He even said that was why the congregation had made me chairman. Everyone knows that about me. And Dave knew it."

"I guess this cover-up thing is too outlandish."

We were both quiet while I finished my beans.

As I walked to the sink to get a glass of water, another thought occurred to me. "There is one other possibility."

"What?"

"Dave still could've been lying about his intentions."

"What intentions?"

"He might not have actually committed adultery. Yet. But he might've been trying, and that would've been easy to cover up."

"That's evil, Jim."

"I know it is, but I have to consider the possibility."

"How could you prove he was trying to seduce Kim?"

"I don't think I can. Intentions, motivations—they're falsifiable. Whether I believe Dave depends on my perspective."

"What do you mean?"

"Well, I can take his story two different ways. Dave might just be in a phase in his marriage, a stage. We've known guys who were dissatisfied in their marriages and it's not easy to find a pattern for how things work out. Take Ron, for example. Starts to feel restricted by his wife. Gets angry and leaves. Then he comes back with his tail between his legs, feels restricted again after a while, and leaves again. Does it three more times before he gets saved and returns for good. But then there's Greg—chairman of the church, keeping up appearances. Stays married in the midst of all his gripes and considers himself a Christian, but secretly carries on an affair with an old girlfriend in another town. Apparently does it for years. Only divorces his wife after it becomes known, and then leaves the church. And I'm the poor sucker who gets stuck with his job. Same kind of unhappiness, opposite trajectories."

"There does seem to be a cold stage in marriage. Like the 'terrible twos.' I could see Dave being in the middle of something like that. We went through it."

"Yeah, and we came out stronger. But the scenario is fluid. If Dave's in it, he could go any number of directions. So far, I've been looking at his story from this perspective, and I figure Dave isn't out there looking for an adulterous relationship."

"You said you could take his story two ways."

"Right. The other is that Dave's not in a phase at all: he's executing a plan. He could be proceeding methodically, not drifting."

"And covering up the plan by lying about his intentions."

"Exactly."

"I get it. But have you ever known a guy who did that? Who destroyed his marriage on purpose?"

"Yes, actually. Remember Bill, my best friend in high school? Married Robin, the ultimate trophy: a beauty, a natural socialite, the sort of woman who attracted rich and influential people. Bill saw Robin as a springboard, nothing more. He used her and his law practice to leap to a higher social stratum. Once he got there, he began to push Robin away, because he despised her. Started with provocations—openly flirting with much younger women. Moved on to casual affairs. After a while, he built up an alternate life—vacations with his other women, houses where his wife wasn't welcome, even cars she couldn't drive. Finally, he paid her off and kicked her out. The most studied exercise in cruelty I've ever seen."

"I remember Robin vaguely. You think Dave might be doing something like that?"

"No, no. Dave couldn't do anything of that magnitude. All I'm saying is, adultery wasn't an impulse for Bill. It was part of a plan. It might be part of a plan for Dave, too. He might be pursuing adultery in a methodical way—for whatever reasons and with whatever resources he has. His conversation with Kim, the drive they took—all that might just be the opening of an adulterous relationship, the necessary prelude. I may have stumbled on the plan before he completed it."

Audrey looked at me and shook her head. "I can't believe we're even thinking these things. We know Dave. Don't we?" She pointed at the phone. "That call I got from Amy yesterday: that was a happy family in the background. Dave can't be planning to cheat on Amy. Even if he is frustrated."

I took her hand. "Now you're wrestling with the same thing I am. I agree with you. I want to believe I can help Dave out of a bad phase in life. But you were also right before. Dave could have lied to me."

Audrey frowned. "If he has, then you haven't done nearly enough yet."

"You're right. I have to make another move. Tonight."

9

Audrey slipped her other hand over mine. "What kind of a move?"

I slid my plate to the side. "That is the question. I have to base my move on Dave's intentions, but I don't know what they are. And I don't think I can discover them, either. So how am I supposed to make a plan?"

"You're making this too complicated, Jim. Just look at his behavior. Doesn't his ride with Kim tell you something?"

"No, it doesn't. It can be explained by both scenarios. A dissatisfied Dave might take the privacy just as much as he would if he were conniving—though for different reasons. The dissatisfied Dave would do it impulsively, without think-ing it might lead somewhere else. The conniving Dave would do it because he might make it lead somewhere else. The fact that he took the car ride doesn't help me prove my case one way or the other."

Audrey thought for a moment. "Well, maybe Dave showed his state of mind while you were talking with him. You must've talked quite a while."

"That's possible." I leaned back in my chair and started to review the conversation again. "Everything he said showed he was negligent, or maybe self-pitying. The way he let himself cross one line after another, the pathetic pleasure he took in their little reunion, the infatuation he felt for who knows how long—all consistent with a disappointed man. Certainly his complaints about Amy fit this story line."

"So, when he said he wanted to get Kim's attention, he was just admitting how wrong he was."

"Maybe. Maybe. But only if his self-pitying statements were the most important ones. He said a lot of other things too. Think about his confession that he wanted privacy with Kim. What if that statement set the context for everything else? Then he was conniving. He maneuvered to get the meeting—which he admitted."

"So all the self-pitying speeches were a smoke screen. I see what you mean. Same conversation, two different interpretations."

"Right. I need some basis for favoring one over the other."

Audrey sulked. "Maybe it doesn't matter. Does it make any difference whether he fell into this situation or jumped? The same events still took place, didn't they? And they might eventually have ended up the same way: an affair. Who cares what motivated him?"

"I care a great deal. His motivations tell me whether he should be a pastor."

"How so?"

"Pastors are men. They struggle with secret desires and disappointments just like everyone else. They go through phases in their marriages. They do stupid things in weak moments. I figure as long as pastors acknowledge their struggles and battle their way to godliness, they have a right to fail sometimes."

"Okay."

"But a predator is different."

"A predator?"

"Yeah. A man who sets out to entice another person into sin, who'll ruin his family to get what he craves—he's not struggling with the normal patterns of life. Sin is his goal. We can't have a predator as our pastor."

"I see what you're saying. So it's not just a matter of helping him deal with this one situation, however bad it might be. You've got to decide whether Dave needs to be fired."

"Exactly."

Audrey shifted in her seat. "Okay, so the question's important. But still, all you have are two theories. If you're going to say our pastor's a predator, you need proof."

"I need a test. Something to clarify which sort of man I'm dealing with, like a clinical trial where I can say, 'If hypothesis A, then the little rat should get fat and happy. If B, then he should keel over dead. All from the same yellow pill.'"

"How do you test Dave's state of mind?"

I raised my finger. "How about this? Dave steps out of the pulpit for a couple of months—two-thirds pay, or whatever. The only public reason is that, after seven years of hard work, he deserves some time for spiritual refreshment. The private reason—so private that it's only stated between Dave, me, and maybe one other man—is that Dave has to make major changes in his marriage. He'll be held to account by me and the other guy, whoever that is, and kept to a course of study and reflection. Maybe counseling would be one of the requirements."

"That's the test?"

"Yeah. I'm pretty sure how a pastor who's in an unhappy phase of his marriage would react to it. He'd probably be hurt, maybe even humiliated at first. He might feel that he'd already given up a lot by confessing so many problems, and that he was being punished unfairly. But if the face-saving element is strong enough, if he's able to make changes without disgrace, he'll eventually see the advantages and get to work. He could even end up grateful."

"All right. But a predator. How would he respond?"

"He might act all insulted and quit. But I'd take it as an admission of guilt, and he'd know that. The guy who gets mad has something at stake. So he'd probably play it cool and try to keep his job. If Dave's a predator, he'd probably go along with the idea to get me off his back, buy a little time. He'd take the sabbatical, undergo the counseling, give the usual lip service, just to string me along. But in the end he'd continue on the same course he had before, toward the same goal—adultery."

"So you'll watch for wounded pride. If Dave shows it, he was probably sincere when he described his motives with Kim. But if he goes along with the sabbatical cooperatively, you'll have the first behavior that doesn't fit the self-pitying, wounded scenario."

"Right. Of course, I'd have to watch carefully. I'd have to hold him to account for how and where he spends his time. He'd have to change his routine—like not going to the Bean at all for the period of the sabbatical, at least. He won't be allowed anywhere near Kim. I'd have to check on the counseling progress. I'd probably be able to discover Dave in the lies he'd have to tell if he's a predator looking for a partner in adultery. In this kind of thing, another trustworthy man will be crucial."

Audrey shook her head. "Sounds like police work, not a lab experiment. I still think you're making this too complicated."

"It's already complicated."

"So don't make it worse."

"How else am I supposed to make a decision? I've got to have more information."

"I know that." She folded her hands.

"I admit my test isn't cut and dried. But at least I'll have more information. And I'll be able to say I did something, that I acted on what I knew."

"True enough." She got up to clear the table.

It was at this point I realized that part of me enjoyed the problem.

It was stimulating to hold a high-stakes matter in my hands. My day-to-day problems at the bank rarely had anything riding on them—bounced checks, personnel troubles, paperwork. But the problem with Dave had huge implications. I had his family, his job, his future in my hands. I had the direction of the church in my hands; the decision of how to deal with this matter was mine, as was the precedent for how to deal with similar stuff in the future.

Beyond that, I enjoyed the sleuthing, the Sherlock Holmes aspect of everything. Audrey was right to call it police work. I'd always considered logic one of my strong suits. I felt I had the ability to untangle complicated, mixed-up situations. I believed I could think beyond my experiences and understand other people. This matter was the right one for me.

And then there was the rush of being responsible for privileged information. In my brain were atomic secrets. A firsthand view of an indiscretion. A direct account of the pastor's marital problems. It was all radioactive. Depending on how I used it, I would be able to grant power to others or withhold it as I saw fit. It was hard to admit to myself, but I found the adrenaline pleasurable, not stressful.

Of course, the rush turned into a bad trip. High stakes were exciting as long as events seemed to break in my favor.

But when they suddenly took a different turn, one that threatened to make me look like an idiot, the high stakes produced anxiety. The sleuthing, too, was good fun as long as part of me could remain detached from the problem. But when the problem demanded all of me, every reserve of strength and passion and integrity, the need for penetrating insight became tyrannical. I couldn't stop sleuthing.

What made the bad trip really bad was the power. I had the secrets, all right. But what had I done with them? Whom had I trusted? Had I made the right calls? Had my sleuthing been thorough enough, unprejudiced enough? It took only a few hours to deplete my power. By the middle of the following morning, I would be helpless. And terrified.

The next evening, parking the car in front of our battered church, watching the other trustees arrive, seeing them shake hands and laugh together, I would know my own helplessness intimately. There was Mike, who'd retired from his title insurance firm. There were Dick and Jake, both retired builders. There was Earl, stumbling out of his car looking worried, every inch a retired hardware retailer, nearly bumping into Tom, a very young UPS driver. And then there was Eddy, the butt of all the jokes, yet always the one who swayed the room. A savvy, retired life insurance man. I would have to hand over the secrets to these men—all the secrets, including my judgment calls. I would have to give them power over me.

There would be nothing left of the rush but the sick urgency of survival. What, after all, could Moses do for forty years except keep pace with the corpses?

But while I digested my dinner and pondered my options, this new inner world was still adventurous. I thought I was a very clever man.

Audrey came back to the table. "What are you going to do now?"

"I'm going to call him, I guess. Start the test."

Rachel appeared. "What test?"

I looked at my watch.

Audrey returned to the sink. "Nothing, Rachel."

"I can keep a secret. You going to fire somebody at the bank, Dad?"

"I don't fire people. I help them discover their talents somewhere else."

"Who are you going to help?"

"Nobody."

"How about Melissa?"

I glared. "How would you know about her?"

Rachel laughed. "Erin told me she was your project this month."

"Flynn doesn't know what she's talking about. No more free lunches for you. Bum off your friends from now on."

Audrey stopped scrubbing. "Melissa. Isn't she the girl with the cleavage?"

Rachel raised her eyebrows. "Oh yeah."

"I told Flynn to write her up for that. And for your information, ladies, Melissa has turned a corner. Another productive member of society, thanks to yours truly."

Audrey looked slyly at Rachel. "So we won't be seeing her on the cover of *Cosmo*?"

"Let's talk about something else."

Audrey looked at me and an edge crept into her voice. "Yes. Let's do. As I recall, dear, you had something to say to your daughter."

I certainly did. I had been curious all day about Rachel's so-called good news. "Your mother says you had some good news yesterday, but she wouldn't tell me what it was. All this time I've been in suspense."

Audrey went back to the sink.

Rachel smiled and looked at her toes. "Yeah."

"Well, come on."

Silence from the sink.

"Pastor Dave asked me to help plan a seminar on courtship for the youth group." She searched me for some sign of pleasure.

My eyes hunted for something plausible to look at. "That's terrific, honey!"

"What's the matter?"

"Nothing's the matter. Isn't this terrific, Audrey?"

More silence from the sink.

"Dad, what's the matter?"

"Nothing. I couldn't be prouder of you."

Rachel smiled, but her lips went slack again. "Thanks."

I stood up and held her by the shoulders. "I mean it, Rachel. You're the perfect young woman to help plan it. You're already setting an example. That makes me very proud. I know you'll do a great job."

She looked at Audrey.

"We're both proud."

She looked back at me, her brows in shallow ridges. "Thanks."

I kissed her and glanced at Audrey. "Thanks for saving my dinner. Gotta go."

I went into the den and shut the door. I put my hand to my forehead and leaned on the bookcase, tempted to pray. But I called Dave instead. He didn't sound too happy to hear from me.

"Dave, you asked me for my help on this marriage stuff, right?"

"Yeah?"

"I've got a prescription for you."

"Can it wait?"

"Not really."

"Okay. Shoot."

"Sabbatical. Two, three months, maybe." It was tempting during the pause that followed to ask, *"Still there? Lungs still working and everything?"* Derek was yelling in the background. "See, I've been thinking about what happened with Kim, and it seems like it went pretty far. An infatuation is fairly serious. I'm very uneasy about it, to tell you the truth. I think there needs to be some intense work on your marriage."

That was probably enough to respond to, so I let another silence sit there. But so did Dave.

"So, I'm recommending this two- or three-month sabbatical. That would give you the time to devote to the issues we talked about. You'd be able to build some satisfaction back into your marriage."

Derek kept yelling. Dave was still silent.

"Of course, I don't think anything should be said to the congregation about all the reasons for it—or even to the trustees, for that matter. I'd just tell them, 'It's been a fruitful seven years for Pastor Dave, and I feel it's time to give him a period of spiritual renewal.' Enough said. That's all the trustees would need to know. But you and I would work on the deeper stuff privately. We might bring one other man into our confidence. And it might be wise for you to get counseling from a fellow pastor."

No breathing yet.

"I'm thinking of a paid sabbatical, naturally. The salary and benefits would continue as usual. You just wouldn't have to preach or keep your discipleship—"

"I never said I was infatuated with Kim."

I seemed to have gotten slightly ahead of him. Too much, too fast. "Well, Dave, maybe not in so many words. But if it was my own conclusion based on what you said, I stand by it. I hope you'll admit you were infatuated—especially admit it to yourself."

"So you can read my mind. You know what's in my heart, is that it?"

"I know what you said about your own thought process. You said you'd dressed up to get her attention. You said you'd let a whole bunch of indiscretions slip by in the conversation with her. And you said that you'd desired the privacy of the car ride with her."

"You're misinterpreting what I said. I thought I could trust you."

"Dave, you're the one who kept bringing the conversation back to your own heart and desires. I wasn't pressing you on that point."

"Look, let's cut to the chase. If you think I'm not qualified to be pastor, you'd better just say so."

"No, not at all—"

"Because I'm not going to be eased out. That's just a way of avoiding the word *fired*."

"No—"

"So if I'm going to be fired, then there's going to be a severance package and the whole deal. I'm not going to be maneuvered into resigning so you and the board can get off easy."

"Dave, stop it!" The pit of my stomach erupted. "You're not going to be fired. You're not going to be maneuvered into resigning. You're not even under suspicion of any sin here, for Pete's sake! You asked for my help, and I'm trying to give it to you. I think you need a sabbatical, and I'm prepared to make the proposal on your behalf."

"I've already asked for more vacation time. I asked for it last April, explicitly so that I could spend more time with my family. I asked for a week. You think I wasn't aware of my problems?"

"I didn't say that. I didn't imply it, either. And I'm not recommending a vacation. I'm recommending work time devoted to your spiritual and family life. I remember your request last spring. It was a good idea, but it obviously didn't go far enough. Let's solve this problem now. That's all I'm saying."

"Jim, I've heard of too many pastors forced out using this kind of sabbatical idea to seriously consider it. Like I said, if you think I'm not fit to be pastor, then that's what you need to say. Don't try to disguise it."

"Dave, that's ridiculous. You're telling me there's no middle ground between saying you're unfit and saying you're perfectly fine to go on pastoring? I'm just saying there's work to do." I needed a breather. "We can't talk about this on the phone. We need to talk face-to-face."

"Let's meet in the morning."

"No. Let's meet right now. Neither of us will get any sleep until we settle this."

"All right, where?"

"The church?"

I stomped down the hall to get my car keys.

So much for my test. The results showed the resistance I'd predicted in a man who was unhappy in his marriage. But the impact felt like the work of a predator. I knew nothing more than I had before the call.

There at the end of the hall was Audrey. "Jim, you're beet red!"

10

It used to take five minutes to get from my house to the church. But that was when McKinley Avenue was called Road 14 and had cows staring at you from behind wire fences, before we knew what Wal-Mart or Home Depot might be. Now, through this stucco canyon of heavily indebted franchises, it takes fifteen minutes door-to-door, no matter what I do—twenty-five when the traffic is bad.

When you're eager to arrive, you rage at the impediments. You only look at the clock to see how late you're going to be.

But when you don't want to arrive, the minutes on the clock become objects of contemplation. You grow fond of them. You delight in how numerous they are. You even dote on them and try to make them stay longer.

Driving to meet Dave, I was only too happy to follow the neighborhood granny through the curves of our development at 20 mph. I not only didn't tailgate, I didn't even have the inclination. Nor did I pass her when we both turned onto McKinley, which is a four-lane road. I didn't get annoyed at the stoplights—not the ones with left-turn signals that take forever; not even the ones that were installed before they came up with those sensors that could detect your car sitting at a red for no good reason. With my stomach being dragged on the road behind me, I was content to watch how long the minutes took to go by.

Still, I was sure the problem was solvable. Dave could still turn. There would be many difficulties—perhaps severe ones. But with persistence, we could keep from throwing this pastor away.

The church was totally dark when I arrived. Apparently Dave was in no big hurry himself. I pulled out my cell and called Flynn. "Sorry to bother you at home."

"No, I'm glad you called. Are you going to stop by and show me your weird clothes?"

"Oh, stop."

"It's past your bedtime."

"Way past."

"So what are you doing?"

"I'm waiting for another meeting."

"You sound stressed."

"Yeah, I guess I am. Say, that new account I initialed this afternoon, the rent-to-own place?"

"What about it?"

"You get all the signature cards from them?"

"Of course. Why?"

"Oh, it's silly."

"I never forget things like that."

"I know. For some reason it just bothered me."

"Was that the only reason you called?"

I paused. "Yeah. Yeah, it was."

"You are stressed. You get bad news this evening? From that other meeting you were going to?"

"This is round two. It's not going well."

"I'm sorry, Jim."

"Well, I shouldn't take your time like this. I'll see you in the morning."

We hung up and I popped a sigh. Dave still hadn't arrived, which probably meant he was explaining to Amy why he had to meet his chairman for the second time in one evening, and why at nine o'clock. That would've been an interesting conversation.

I wondered if Dave used the same power plays on her that he used on the rest of us. Did she put up with it? Or did she just stare him down with that ironic face and make him feel ridiculous? Maybe he didn't even try.

He'd certainly tried with me—successfully, and not for the first time.

Yes, Dave was a likable guy. Yes, he was a persuasive preacher. He did have a wonderful, even exceptional, family. And he was insightful about people.

But those same qualities had other facets—like the one I encountered again during our phone call. He had levers to make people respond the way he wanted. And the less responsive people were, the more active the levers became.

In preaching, his levers tended to be emotional—which is typical of many pastors. For every sermon, he had a stock of moving anecdotes: the poor kid in bombed-out London in 1945, drooling as he looks through the window of the pastry shop—and the drooling gets sloppier with every telling—and the American soldier who buys doughnuts for the kid, who responds by asking, "Mister, are you God?" It wasn't my cup of tea, but the ladies would cry pretty much every Sunday, and I suppose Dave's dramatic abilities were what kept people coming.

But if for some reason Dave saw that the sermon wasn't working—the ladies weren't crying, or the teens were slumped in their seats sending text messages—he'd move the ultimate lever. He'd start to cry himself—typically toward the end. He'd tell one last story and break down as he delivered the punch line: "And suddenly the auction was over. The auctioneer explained that the wealthy man had stipulated in his will that all his fortune, all the art treasures in his collection [choke], would go to the one who bought that portrait of his [choke] son—to the one [rasp] who honored his son." Then the ladies would cry.

Dave's graciousness, admirable though it was, had an element of control too. His graciousness to Dad, for instance, was impressive, but the Kool-Aid of mercy was spiked with flattery. Dave sensed Dad's professional pique waiting to explode and tried to soothe it. He'd do more than consult Dad on financial matters. He'd say, "I wish there were a dozen more men like you in the church," or, "If people would only listen to you, things would go a lot smoother." It worked. Dad thought Dave was the best pastor we'd ever had. Of *course* he was softening.

Had Dave's charming family been produced by something beyond love and discipline? Was it control? Were they that good, or were they passive?

One evening, I'd had to drop some paperwork by their house, but I hadn't said exactly when I would show up. When I arrived, and Amy opened the door, the atmosphere seemed awkward. The kids weren't playing, just sitting on the couch with their legs bouncing nervously on the cushion, their heads down. Amy herself seemed uncharacteristically at a loss. Then Dave came sailing through the living room, unaware that I was at the door. When he saw me, he swung around good-naturedly and smiled, and by his demeanor you'd never think anything was wrong. But the skin under his eyes was dark and veins stuck out on his neck. I didn't stay.

His intuitive knowledge of people certainly was put to good use. He had spared Agnes Thurman a lot of unnecessary anger and embarrassment by distracting her before she could hear Mike's "awful carpet" comment. He must've headed off a thousand conflicts that way.

But his intuition just added more levers to his control panel. For every Agnes who was spared embarrassment by Dave's insight, there was a Dorothy who was put on the spot.

Dorothy Baumgartner had many opinions, especially on the subject of music. For her, a new song was anything written after 1945, and the "good old hymns" were those written during the 1920s and 30s. She often mistook hymns written before then for new ones. She'd been the church organist before the not-very-sure-footed Pastor Harvey had announced that all music in the morning service would now be geared to twenty-five-year-olds. Dorothy considered herself fired. Pastor Harvey didn't last long, but we never got Dorothy back to the organ, not even for an offertory. As far as anyone knew, she quit playing entirely.

Her bitterness gave an edge to everything she said about music. She'd tell Dave that the band was too loud, the singers too soft, the choruses too repetitious, and the "old hymns" too fast. The edge was in her choice of words: "that rock group," "those crooners," and "those ditties." Some of us wondered whether Dorothy came to church only to see if the lightning would finally strike.

During one evening meeting, Dorothy got the floor and began what seemed like a relatively mild version of her music speech, delivered this time not as a harangue but as a plea from the silent but patient majority for more of the "old hymns." In spite of Dorothy's attempt to soften her tone, Dave jumped up to the microphone, smiled real big, and cut her off. "Dorothy, you know you've got a standing invitation to share your organ music with us in the worship service anytime you want. I wish you'd take us up on it."

The effect on the room was something to behold. The older folks smiled and applauded. Some of the ladies even said, "Oh yes, Dorothy, please!" The younger people also applauded, but gave each other glances swollen with admiration for their pastor's craftiness. Dorothy herself just sat down muttering.

Dave's ploy was skillful. Dorothy never attended another meeting. But it was also a cheap use of a divided house. A woman already bitter over being mistreated didn't deserve it, whatever her abrasiveness.

Dave's power plays also included two that outmaneuvered me.

In the middle of our honeymoon period with Dave, he and the trustees were loafing in the conference room on the pretext that it was the third Wednesday of the month, their scheduled meeting. The air was close and the collars loose. The odor of sawdust, which had penetrated Jake's sweat glands after a lifetime of building houses, overpowered the familiar smell of scorched coffee.

Greg, then chairman, had called the meeting to order and we'd approved the minutes. An hour later, that remained the only business decided.

How we got to Eddy's story about selling life insurance to Madame Ruby, our local psychic, I no longer recall. But Eddy was being his marvelous poker-faced self. "So I start down the questionnaire. What's your full name? Can't put Madame Ruby on the form. What's your address, age, height? Then I have to ask her weight."

Dick howled. "You guys ever seen Madame Ruby?"

Greg was convulsed. "Did you have a big enough chair, Eddy?"

"Let's just say we hunted for one without armrests."

Jake recovered himself. "So you asked her weight . . ."

"I asked, and she flat refused to answer."

Mike, Dick, and Jake were in tears. Greg doubled over. Earl smiled and Dave shook his head.

Eddy waited. "So I says, 'Lady, the company has to be able to weigh the risks.'"

"You said that?"

"Weigh the risks!"

"She says, 'What risks?' So I back up. 'Look at it from the company's point of view,' I says. 'They have to make money, right? They don't just pay benefits out of the goodness of their hearts. They're betting you pay enough premiums before you die.'"

All eyes on Eddy.

"She goes white. She starts scrambling, like she's lost her purse. So I ask her, 'What's the matter?' And she says, 'You said that word, so I have to knock on wood.'"

"She said that?"

"Knock on wood!"

"I tell her she can knock on my desk, but she says, 'No, that's laminate.'"

Deafening hysterics.

"So now we're both hunting around for a piece of wood . . ."

It was that kind of meeting.

There was no topping Eddy, so when the last man wheezed his last laugh, Greg leaned back. "Any business to talk about?"

Amid the hesitant murmuring, Dave made his move. "Actually, guys, I've been thinking. One way to make things run a little smoother in the office would be to make me a signer on the church accounts. Then if we have some surprise like that spotlight rental last week, I can just take care of it. I mean, Eddy had to leave the Doughnut Hole and come all the way down here just to sign one measly check."

Yuk, yuk, yuk.

Dick stuck his elbow into Eddy's paunch. "That Eddy's got to have his glazed doughnut or he gets headaches."

Yuk, yuk, yuk.

Jake leaned over the table. "Maybe Eddy's wife just wants an hour's peace."

Yuk, yuk.

"Hey, my doughnut time's for witnessing. That whole pagan gang is down there every day. Somebody's got to shine the light in the darkness!"

Yuk, yuk.

I won't get started on the spotlight rental, which was an early instance of Dave's renting equipment that neither he nor anyone else knew how to use. Nor will I get started on the total financial impropriety of a pastor being a signer on church accounts, on the temptations it exposes him to, or on the stupidity of any pastor who takes responsibility for spending the offerings. I won't describe the apoplectic fit Dad threw when he found out that the board had indeed made Dave a signer and that his banker son sat there like a bump on a log. I'll especially forbear reporting his speech about how his son was now one of the insiders who didn't think being straight with the congregation was important.

Greg looked around the table. "Thoughts?"

Mike, Dick, and Jake looked back and forth between Eddy and each other.

I shifted in my seat. "Um, convenience aside, being a signer exposes you to accusations, Dave. I think Eddy can be released from witnessing at the Doughnut Hole occasionally."

Polite yuks.

Greg continued looking around. If no one intervened, my comment would be the end of it. Going. Going.

"Still." Eddy shrugged. "There's a lot going on."

Dick nodded.

Jake tugged his mouth to one side as if acknowledging a painful truth. "Sure is."

Mike folded his arms and looked away from me. "Besides, I hate rules and regulations."

Eddy looked up. "We can trust Dave, can't we, Jim?"

Dave's use of that meeting was masterful. He not only showed an effortless control over those men, he gained more control in the bargain. More rentals, moving on to purchases, which gradually increased in magnitude. And nobody could stop him. Outside the meetings, Mike and Earl would grouse about his spending, but nobody ever considered curtailing or revoking his privilege.

Dave later advanced his control over the business side of the church a significant step further.

The church was trying to buy land. The neighborhood around us had become jammed with cheaply constructed houses. There was warped T-111 siding as far as the eye could see in every direction. It didn't take very many years before our street was cluttered with broken-down cars, all dripping oil. With two services and a parking mess, it was time to move.

The board had looked at various parcels on the edges of town. One sold before it got listed. Another was zoned wrong and nobody wanted to rely on the city's goodwill—smart, because there wasn't any. Another seemed to be exactly right—so right that the seller got a whiff of the tens of thousands of dollars more he might get. He kept following his nose and raising the price until we realized the deal stunk.

A move wasn't looking too promising until Dave remembered an old friend of his dad's. This friend, a guy named Hank Wagner, owned thirty acres visible from the freeway and near an exit. It was in an undeveloped area within city limits and had the right zoning. Water, sewer, and gas were close. Just one problem: it wasn't on the market, and we doubted we could afford the potential asking price.

One evening, the trustees were trying to figure out what to do—Dave, myself, five men long retired, and one very young UPS driver who was totally inexperienced in land deals and said so repeatedly. The decision-making process was glacial. None of the trustees knew this Hank Wagner or had any connection with his family, which seemed to be an insurmountable obstacle to the old guys, especially Jake.

"How can we do business with a man nobody's ever heard of?"

Finally, I got frustrated. "Look, guys, you don't have to know people anymore. Nobody knows anyone in this town now. Just call Hank Wagner up and ask if he'll sell and what he'd take for the parcel." This at least set the discussion onto grinding a new pile of rocks—as in, who should call Hank? Should Dick? Mike? Earl?

Dave chose this point to cut in. "Why don't you let me call him?" Except for Earl murmuring "I don't know" and peering at the others, there was an icy silence, so Dave went on. "Hank knows me. He and Dad go way back, like I said before, and they've never had any bad blood. Let me call him. Let me negotiate with him and see how far we get."

Another silence.

I was now chairman and I didn't have to allow dead time. "Dave, I appreciate your willingness to jump in and move this thing along. We really need that kind of initiative. But I don't think the pastor should be the one to make this call. In general, I think it's better for you to continue devoting your time to spiritual things rather than business. Real estate deals in particular can be pretty dicey. You don't want the responsibility if things turn out badly. It would hurt your ministry, Dave."

But Mike had other ideas. "Yeah, Jim, but we laymen don't always do the best job with these things. Just remember that awful carpet we had downstairs for years. A layman chose that. And, anyway, Dave's got the connection. This man Hank knows him, watched how he's turned out, trusts his dad. Why not let Dave at least try?"

Tom shrugged his shoulders. Eddy nodded, and so did Dick, Jake, and finally Earl.

Another masterful exhibition of control. Dave knew the old guys' nostalgia for the days when there were fewer pages in transactions and more fleshy handshakes, when you could laugh your way through business. Dave made the call.

In the end, it seemed to work out well. The church paid $900,000 for the parcel. A pretty favorable deal—undoubtedly the result of Dave's close connection and persuasive charms.

Everyone agreed the church had been very well served by this approach, and I ate crow.

But it wasn't the short-term results that bothered me, it was the control. As Dave finally rounded the corner, parked, and walked into the church, I wondered whether it wasn't time to talk about that control.

II

We were silent for a while sitting in the bare, windowless conference room with scratched-up walls, battleship-gray carpet, frayed in one corner, and the fluorescent overhead lights buzzing. It smelled like sweaty teenagers.

"Where were we, Jim?"

I paused before yielding up my silence, thinking, I guess, that it would heighten the drama. "I think where we were, Dave, was you weren't liking my suggestions and I was feeling manipulated. I think that's where we were."

"I definitely wasn't liking your suggestions."

"Well, what do you expect me to do, Dave? Seriously! What do you expect me to do? My pastor gets infatuated with some old high school friend and gets in her Mercedes to go for a private drive. My pastor tells me he's unhappy in his marriage and he doesn't respect his wife. And it's not like I'm an impartial observer. I'm the chairman of the church board. I have responsibilities. I'm supposed to do something when I hear things like this from the pastor. If you don't like my suggestions, that's fine. I'm not crazy about your behavior."

"You make it sound like adultery."

"How am I supposed to know it wasn't? When you really stop and think about it, how am I supposed to know you haven't covered anything up? You told me you wanted to get in Kim's car. You told me about your marriage. I'd have to be an idiot not to at least consider whether you've covered up an affair. Or are headed into one."

"So you do think I'm committing adultery."

"I have no way of knowing, Dave. I believe you told me the truth about yesterday, but only because no liar would be crazy enough to tell so much if he wasn't forced to. I'm making a bet, not an inference. What else did you want to do with Kim? I don't even know enough to bet. I'm saying you need a sabbatical, because I can't do any less and I'm not prepared to go further. You can use a sabbatical to prove yourself—to me."

I became more disconcerted as I talked, not because I doubted my reasoning but because of Dave's detachment. There was not the smallest tic of defensiveness in his body. In fact, the further I went, the more relaxed he became—lips releasing their compression, eyelids dropping subtly, jaw unclenching. I wasn't exactly softening my position, but he was unfazed.

So I got louder. "The way you manipulate just makes this whole thing harder to figure out. You did that song and dance on the phone about being fired when I hadn't said a word about it. That was a power play. You were trying to make me defend a position I hadn't taken, pretending I had ulterior motives and making me try to prove otherwise. I'm sick of your games."

"I don't understand. You'll have to give me another example of my games. I don't think I've ever talked about being fired before."

"I can give you any number of other examples, like what you did to Dorothy Baumgartner. Inviting her to play the organ when you knew she wouldn't—in front of the whole congregation. You humiliated her. And you got away with it because you tricked the older people. But the younger people saw exactly what you did, and they admired you because they wanted her to shut up. That's what I'm talking about. Control."

Silence. Nothing. No fear, no anger.

"Or take the way you grabbed the church's money. You had those old guys wrapped around your little finger. You got them to make you a signer on the accounts by teasing Eddy about doughnuts. If they'd thought about why no pastor had ever been a signer in the whole history of the church, they never would've given you the privilege. You made sure they didn't think.

"It was the same when you got the authority to negotiate with Hank Wagner. You played on their nostalgia. You exploited their dependency on personal connections. You used their helplessness and impotence to get them to do something they'd never do if they thought about the implications. It was another control maneuver."

Dave's voice was as serene as April air. "So, Jim, this is really about the land deal. You didn't want me to handle it—and I respect that, I really do. There are definitely reasons why a pastor shouldn't interfere in the business affairs of the church. But it seems like you resent my success."

Even amid the exhilaration of releasing my stored-up resentment, I could see I'd been a fool. But there was no turning back now. "Dave, this isn't politics. There's no audience to impress. Only me."

"I don't know why you think I'm playing to an audience. I'm talking about our relationship. You've obviously been keeping a record of wrongs against me. That's what I'm talking about. You should've confronted me about these things when they happened, like Matthew 18 says. Instead, you allowed a root of bitterness in your heart. I think we need to deal with that. I think you've misunderstood my motivations in all these cases. I don't want control."

"Then why did you humiliate Dorothy? What was that maneuver about, if not control?"

"I didn't humiliate her. I invited her to play the organ. That wasn't about control. It was about asking a negative person to be part of the solution instead of the problem. I don't see what's wrong with that."

"I can give you at least three things that are wrong with it. For one thing, I happen to know you hate organ music. I've heard your imitation of the warble. It's very funny, especially the air-organ finger motions. Your invitation was insincere. That's what was wrong with it. More than that, I happen to know Dorothy got under your skin. You ranted to me about her complaints after more than one meeting. You took them personally, and you said you wished she'd shut up—in so many words. You had no right to humiliate her in retaliation for feeling personally attacked. It was wrong.

"But the most important thing was your manipulation of the congregation. You gave that invitation knowing it would be approved by both young and old, but for very different reasons. You played to the self-satisfaction of both groups. And you did it to divide them, which only compounds the wrong. The very idea that you were asking Dorothy to be part of the solution is laughable."

"You're reading an awful lot into what I said."

"Okay, then why did you want to be a signer?"

"As I said at the time, it just made sense. It was more convenient."

"For you."

"Well, yes, but also for guys like Eddy."

"Aw, come on. If you had really cared about Eddy's time, you would've planned ahead to rent that spotlight. You would've gotten it done a couple weeks in advance. You didn't do that because you didn't think about the hassle it would be for Eddy. But suddenly Eddy's time becomes important when it serves as an excuse for you to be a signer.

"Being a signer allows you the luxury of procrastination, when we both know you have the ability and the discipline to think ahead. It also allows you to buy stuff without having to justify it to the board. It's not about respecting the trustees' time. It's about control."

Dave's voice was cool, his inflection nonchalant. "Here again, you're using the least charitable interpretation of my motives. You could've given me some credit."

"What other interpretation can there be? How else am I supposed to reconcile all the inconsistencies between the facts of each event and the rationalizations you give afterward? If this is the least charitable interpretation, it's not the one I had at first. I came to it reluctantly, over seven years. Maybe manipulation is so much a part of your personality that you aren't even conscious of it. But I don't think that's any more charitable."

"Jim, look. I can't change the way you read my motives. I think your opinion of me is driven by jealousy, and until you deal with it you're going to keep harboring these grudges."

"I think the problem is your behavior. I haven't once taken the least charitable view of your actions today. If I had, we wouldn't even be talking right now. Your conduct looked so bad, I could've found reasons to take it straight to the board tonight, if I'd wanted to. If I weren't doing my best to be gracious, I wouldn't have suggested a sabbatical at all. You'd just be fired."

His tone was sweet with regret. "See, it's that kind of statement that I'm talking about. You seem to think you have a huge amount of authority in this church. You judge my motives, and then you act like your opinions will sway everybody else's. You apparently think you've got all the power. Frankly, I don't know whether I want your help with Amy."

"You are not responding to what I've been saying. You are pretending that you can still set the terms for this conversation. You are ignoring the extent of your problems. You are trying to switch the focus onto my motives. Your behavior right now is an example of your control tactics. You are damaging your position with me every time you open your mouth."

"You aren't my judge. Do I have problems? Yes. Do I need to deal with them? Certainly. But you judge me as if you know my motivations. You don't have the authority to do that."

My stomach erupted again. "It's not a matter of judging you, Dave. It's not a matter of reading your motivations, or grading the charitableness of my interpretations, or restraining my apparently insatiable lust for power. I am the chairman of the church. I have responsibilities. Your maneuvering does nothing to change that."

"The board has responsibilities, not you alone."

"I lead the board. I will recommend how to deal with you. I will determine how much everyone knows about what you did today. I saw your breach of decorum. I've heard your statements. The board hasn't. Yet. And after having been jerked around for the last half hour, I am in no mood to help you out. I do not trust you."

. His body was loose even now that I'd made the bottom line explicit. How could Dave fight so hard without any sweat? Without any apparent sense of danger?

Dave let some seconds tick by. He finally answered me without a sigh or even a cringe of irritation. "I know you don't trust me, Jim. That's what I've been saying. You've been interpreting my motives through your own jealousy. I can't change that. Only you can. I'm saying you have to let go of your need to be in the driver's seat and deal with your feelings."

That was it.

"Dave, I'm done here. You are the problem, not me. So this is where we stand: You got into a car with a woman who's not your wife. You did it, according to your own account, because you desired that kind of privacy. I have to do something about that. I can't leave it alone. So I want you to take a sabbatical. I don't want it because I know your heart. I want it because I *don't* know your heart. I have no other way of meeting my responsibilities to the church and being fair to you at the same time. If you cooperate with me, you'll have plenty of opportunity to prove yourself. You can prove your love for Amy and you can prove your fitness to be pastor. I'm only too happy to see that happen.

"But through our whole conversation on the phone and here in this room, I have seen a level of manipulation that frustrates and dismays me. You claim I'm motivated by jealousy. That is the very kind of judgment you accuse me of making. It is a hypocritical power play, a politician's attempt to change the subject. It's a betrayal of my trust.

"So in order for this sabbatical to work, you have to relinquish control, starting now. You will not dictate how this process goes, and you won't be able to manipulate it. Your ability to take direction will be the primary indicator to me that you're sincere. Any more control maneuvers on your part will signal to me that you're not trustworthy.

"That's where we stand."

Dave didn't smirk. The look on his face didn't even approach a smirk. If I'd taken a photo of him at that moment, you wouldn't see any cockeyed grin. But his confidence smirked. His serenity, the way his body leaned in the chair, replied with mockery.

"So if I cooperate with you on this sabbatical, I am giving up all control over the process. You're pretty much going to dictate the whole thing."

"Right."

"And if I try to assert control, you will conclude that my cooperation is insincere. You'll think I'm going along with you as a cover-up, or to buy time or something."

"Right."

"What if I don't cooperate, sincerely or insincerely?"

I smiled. "I will tell the board both what you did with Kim yesterday and how you resisted me this evening. I'll tell them what you said about your marriage. And I'll argue that you need to be fired. I'll do all those things not because I know your heart, but because I don't know it. And you'll have to take your chances."

12

I heard the music rise. I loved my line. I loved my delivery. I loved the unease that started in Dave's hands. I loved how it stiffened his shoulders. And I especially loved his studied expression, that sincerity move he did with his lips.

I saw extreme close-ups of his eyes, their lids pulled back and their pupils reaching. Cut to me, reclining and fixing Dave with a ruthless stare. And then a shot from the ceiling, capturing the posture of the antagonists, the one rigid and the other easy. The ceiling cam pans around the two. Cue bass drums and low brass. Cue mournful oboe.

Close-up on Dave as he shakes his head slowly, never taking his eyes off Jim. Move in tight on the mouth beginning to open.

And, table cam, get ready for the sag, when his torso falls into his belly and his shoulders slump and his little backward-slanted chin disappears into the flesh of his neck. Wait for it! Wait! Now! See his T-shirt wad up, the dippy crew neck hang loose, and the "Got Jesus?" letters fold over each other.

Cue horns! Cue trumpets!

Cut to Jim, the resolve on his face now softened with magnanimity that shines like a tear. Cue soft light behind his face. He leans in. His muscular forearm, bronzed and gleaming, extends across the table. Close-up on Jim's rough, open hand.

Cue violin. Fade to black.

The problem was, it really happened that way, Dave showing each gesture to my vanity with a truthfulness worthy of the Actors Studio.

It happened, that is, except for the magnanimity bit. My hand was not open. I knew the gracious winner was a role I had played often and well. I knew I could play it again if I wanted. But I had trouble wanting to. Besides, I wondered who was lying more by this time, Dave or me?

He rubbed the back of his neck. "Look, Jim, my emotions have run away with me. I've antagonized you. I've been reacting to you like a cornered animal. You're not out to get me. I know that. But this whole thing has been deeply embarrassing, as you can imagine."

"I can imagine it, but you've got to get a grip."

"You're right—"

"It doesn't matter how embarrassing this is. You've got a lot of serious responsibilities."

"You're absolutely right."

"It's time to be an adult."

Something flashed inside his eyes. "I think I get it now. I see where you're coming from."

"Good."

"I was feeling judged before, but now I hear you."

"Feeling judged? How do you think I felt?"

"Judged."

"Yeah. I'm not jealous of you."

"I know. It was unfair of me to say that. You're just saying you thought you knew my heart, but since yesterday you're not so sure."

"Right. That's what I've been saying this whole time."

Brow unfurrowed, face lowered. "I'm your pastor, but you don't know my heart. How can you have any confidence in my ministry if you don't know whether I'm genuine, whether I'm the man I claim to be?"

"Exactly."

"That's pretty serious, Jim. It doesn't get more basic than that."

"No, I guess it doesn't."

"I apologize. I shouldn't have accused you of judging me. I knew you better than that, I really did. And I shouldn't have said you were jealous over the land deal. That was pretty low. You've been trying to help me this whole time and I've been resisting you. I'm sorry."

My heart was finally beating normally. "That's okay, Dave. I can understand your resistance. I even expected it. You've been forthright about very hurtful stuff tonight, and I knew the sabbatical was going to seem like a punishment. It's really not, though. It's about moving forward."

"I see that now." Deep breath, hands braced on the knees. Face up, lips compressed. "But I think I need to resign. I think that's the only honorable thing to do."

Why is it that we fall for the same deceptions over and over? How many sighs of regret does it take before we stop being simple? Couldn't I learn?

Not with my ambitions.

I can hear the loud voices in the meetings; I can see the exasperated turns away, the shaking heads, the murmuring women. I can hear the rustle of the widow standing up behind me after another despairing adjournment and saying to no one in particular, "It happened again. We let it happen again." I can feel the strain of being a cheerful boy in a silent car, trying to think how I could make Dad laugh before we arrived home. I can envision my mother's neck, stiff as a flagpole, her head held with her chin tucked down, facing directly at the windshield as she said, "Go by yourself next time." These scenes repeated quarterly all the way into my teenage years—first minus my mother, then minus my brother, and then minus me.

What was so dishonorable about wanting to change that way of doing business?

If the problem was anger, both pent-up and released, then the solution had to be grace, stored and distributed. It seemed a straightforward enough deduction. What was selfish or vainglorious about wanting to be the gracious leader who would build the storehouse and organize the disbursements? It would take love and self-control to become that leader, not ruthlessness or strategy.

I thought my ambitions were the same ones Jesus had.

How would Jesus have reacted when Greg's affair was exposed? When Dave went to see Greg, I went along. Greg opened the door with a smile. With a smile he told us how happy he was with his mistress. With a smile he evaded our pleas to change his ways. It was a sickening, likeable performance. Even in the face of the clearest sin, I forced my hand out and shook Greg's. I looked him in the eye with respect. I didn't throw him away.

That's what I thought Jesus would have done.

So now I refused to throw Dave away. I couldn't sidestep this opportunity to show the church how grace was done.

"I think I need to resign, Jim. I think that's the only honorable thing to do."

"No, no, Dave."

"Jim, I've lost your confidence. A pastor needs to move on when he loses his chairman's confidence."

"No, wait."

"And the thing is, I can see now that I've lost it through my own fault, not yours. I can't blame you, and I don't."

"Dave, hold on, you haven't lost my confidence."

"How can you say that? I certainly have, and if I were in your shoes, I'd feel exactly the way you do."

"No, look. I got angry and I went too far in a lot of the things I said. I shouldn't have allowed that to happen. Please don't read too much into it."

"That's very gracious of you, Jim. It's right in character, because you're a gracious guy. But I was pretending to read your motivations, and that's very hurtful. When you pile that on top of what I did yesterday, I can understand your anger. I can see your point. How can you know whether I'm genuine after a day like this?"

I sighed and leaned on my elbows. "Let me try to explain this, Dave. It's very important to me that you not resign.

"I've been in this church since I was a baby. I've seen how every pastor has been treated for the past four decades. We've punished them for every little imperfection. No surprise: that's how we've treated each other. We've been spiteful, angry, bitter—we've been this way my whole life.

"If you resign, it will be one more punishment meted out to one more pastor.

"We have to stop this. Whatever you've done has to be corrected in a gracious way. You're not perfect, and none of our pastors has been. So you have to learn from me, not cower. That kind of change takes work—from both of us. I need to exercise understanding and you need to exercise discipline. We both need to grow. If you resign, none of these essential things will be done—not in you, not in me, and not in the church. We won't learn. We'll just blunder along."

We were silent for a while, listening to the lights buzzing.

My elbows seemed to be pulled back into my sides. "I won't deny that I'm having a lot of trouble with this whole thing. I said I don't trust you. I guess I can't take it back or revise it. But what I'm trying to say is that it's not final. I want to regain trust. Your resigning just leaves everything unresolved."

"It's easier to resign."

"What do you mean? How can it be easier to quit your job, put your family through all that stress, lose all that time and money, and find another position? How is that easier than learning and growing?"

"If I resign I don't have to humble myself. But I will have to if I want to learn. It's easier to give up a life here than it is to give up my pride. Pretty sad."

The mystery was not how Dave could have lied so comprehensively. When it was all over, I understood his lying—his reasons, his methods. What I could not understand was how he could make such true statements with such sincerity. How could he be so sunk in sin and still say something sounding so right?

I leaned back in my chair. "I see what you're saying. But if you stay you won't be alone. I'll have to humble myself before you, too."

Dave picked at the chipped veneer on the table. He finally looked up. "Okay. Let's do a sabbatical. I'll stay."

The music swelled again. Horns, violins, the works. His moist eyes were more moving to me because they never quite overflowed. His light sniffle worked well too—as if he were covering tears, not wallowing. He kept picking at the veneer while I tried to contain my elation by staring at a black scrape on the wall. By now my nose had been deadened to the stale sweat, but I imagined fresh air had seeped through a crack.

Finally I stirred. "We're on a roll. Can we fix any other calamities?"

Dave laughed. "How about the West Bank and Gaza?"

"Sure! I got time."

We both sighed.

Dave looked at me. "We do need to work out the financial arrangements, Jim. We don't have a lot of wiggle room in our budget."

"Like I said earlier, I'll propose that you continue at full salary. You still have a house payment to make. I can't guarantee the trustees will go for it, but I don't think it'll be a problem."

"How long are we talking about?"

"I don't know. What do you think? Some of the issues are pretty serious."

"Too serious for a sabbatical."

"Maybe so. But how long do you think it'll take to lay a foundation for growth with Amy? Restore some confidence?"

"Three months?"

"Okay, three months. What are we going to have you do for three months? Reading books about marriage isn't what I had in mind. I think there has to be some counseling."

"Yeah, you're probably right. I don't like it, but you're probably right. I can ask around at the seminary if someone there would be willing to take this on. There are a couple of profs I really trust, and it's not too far a drive. Speaking of which, am I supposed to leave town?"

"For part of the time, at least." I realized now how superficial my thinking had been. How was I going to hold him accountable if he was out of town? How was he supposed to pay for it? "Maybe there's some sort of residency you can do at the seminary."

"Maybe. I can ask about it."

"I'll factor some dollars into my proposal to house you, at least for a while. I do think while you're home you should stay away from the Bean."

"I don't like that."

"I'm sorry, but that's the way it goes."

"You think I'd feed an infatuation with Kim or something by going there?"

"You'd have more opportunities to talk with her. That relationship needs to be cut off so you can focus exclusively on Amy."

"Cut off without explanation?"

"Just don't be available anymore. Don't go to the coffee shop. There's nothing to explain."

Dave shook his head. "I really don't like it."

"Dave, this is going to be a tough process. Not going to the Bean is just the beginning, and it's not a large issue compared to the others. I'm not saying you'll never see the place again."

"I know. But I'm not in love with Kim. I haven't lost all my self-control."

"I'm not saying you've lost your self-control. The issue isn't that you're too focused on Kim. The issue is you're not focused on Amy. Just stay away from the Bean. It'll help change your perspective."

Dave looked away. "You're asking me to do it, so I'll do it. Maybe I'll understand it later."

"Fair enough."

We eased back into business mode, leaving the tangle of sensitive issues behind for the clear, free road of money. We knocked out questions from rent to the cost of counseling. But then Dave veered back into the thickets.

"What are you going to tell Amy?"

Hadn't thought about that. She was bound to share Dave's fear of being eased into resignation. She would at least wonder why I proposed the sabbatical. Did I have to tell her what Dave had done? About the drive he took? About all the confessions he'd made? "I don't think I should tell her anything. You need to tell her whatever you think is right. I'm not going to snitch on you, if that's what you're asking."

"That's fine, but I'm in a difficult position. She's already wondering what we've been talking about tonight. If I come home saying we're going to take a sabbatical, she's going to worry that something's wrong. What do you want me to tell her? Do you want me to tell her I took a drive with Kim and you saw it?"

"This is really out of my league."

"Well, I have to tell her something."

"Maybe you should confess what you confessed to me—a poor attitude. Tell her I thought you should deal with it, and this sabbatical was the method we came up with."

"Poor attitude? About what?"

"About marriage, the kids, life in general. I don't know."

"That's going to open a whole lot of questions."

"Yeah, it will. But that's what this is all about. You'll have to bring up the state of your marriage eventually."

"By telling her I had a great conversation with another woman? I don't want her to think the worst."

"She doesn't have to think the worst."

"So don't tell her about Kim?"

"I don't know, Dave. I don't know where the line is between deceit and diplomacy on this one. I'm not the guy to advise you."

"I don't want to tell her."

"I'm not saying you should and I'm not saying you shouldn't. I'm saying get some advice from somebody who knows something about this. I can't help you."

"All right. I'll get some advice."

I watched him go back to picking at the veneer. "Let me know who you talk to."

"Okay."

"And what they say."

"Yeah."

The lights buzzed relentlessly. We'd done all we could to flesh out the idea, yet we continued to sit there. I whacked a cheap pen on the side of the table.

Dave sighed. "As hard as it is, I'll be glad to get out of town for a while. We definitely need some family time away."

"Wait a minute. Wait. Time away together? You asked for extra vacation time last spring. What did you do with that week? Why didn't you guys go away together?"

13

D ave stared blankly. "What do you mean why didn't we go away together?"

"You took the extra week you asked for, but you didn't take it with Amy and the kids. Back then, you said you needed the family time. Why didn't you take it?"

"What are you talking about? I'm confused."

"You asked for more vacation time last spring, right?"

"Right."

"You asked for a week."

"Yeah."

"You took that week within a month of requesting it. I remember how fast it was because you had to line up a couple of missionary speakers on short notice and you told me how difficult it was. We ended up throwing together a missions conference around those two speakers and almost burned out the missions committee. It was a pain in the neck to get it done that quickly, but I figured you badly needed the week with your family. I could see why you needed it, as busy as you'd been."

"I remember all that."

"So why didn't you go somewhere together?"

"I still don't follow you. We took the week."

"Yes, but you didn't take it together. Before you left, I asked you where you were going. Remember? We were sitting right here after some meeting, talking about nice vacations our families had taken, and I said, 'So where are you going?' You said, 'Chicago.' And then we talked about Chicago and all the fun stuff to do there."

"Right, but I still don't follow you."

"Well, when I asked you how the week had been, you said the Sears Tower was great and the Magnificent Mile was fun, but it was too cold."

"Yeah."

I let him dangle there for a second or two. "Dave, Amy called Audrey from her mother's house that week. She said she couldn't remember whether she'd locked the back door to the house and asked Audrey to check it. Audrey thought it was odd, because I'd told her all about your exciting vacation to Chicago, yet here was Amy saying she'd gotten to Fresno without knowing if she'd locked her door. I've never heard of anybody from here going to Chicago by way of California."

Dave laughed real hard. "Oh! I completely misunderstood! I can see why that threw you. I went to Chicago for a couple of days that week, but then joined Amy and the kids at her mother's. I'm sorry! I got totally turned around."

I laughed too, somewhat less heartily. "So what were you doing in Chicago?"

He was settling down now. "Oh, there was a conference I wanted to attend."

"A conference?"

"Yeah. Willow Creek was putting on a two-day thing about worship, and I didn't want to miss it."

"I see. How was it?"

"Fantastic. All of their conferences are top-notch."

"Why was it so important?"

"I get such a blessing from the music. It's totally professional: no sound-system troubles, no women screeching out the high notes, no taped accompaniment to the vocalists. They have unbelievable talent in that church. Just unbelievable. The singers all have studio-quality voices and they memorize their songs. Then they have drama teams, which are hilarious. Those people could be on TV. The skits illustrate the points that the speaker will make that day, so they add a lot to the worship."

"So what did you learn?"

"Well, there were workshops on the how-tos of stage production, sound, lighting, getting the music right. I got a lot of ideas for our new building, that's for sure. When we build, we need to design the platform for drama, with the lighting technology and the sound system worked into the budget. It will make our whole experience much more powerful, more like what people see in their ordinary lives. People are used to a lot of technology now—PowerPoint at the office, digital animation at the movies, computer games in their homes. We need to use more technology in our Sunday morning program, just to be relevant to where people are at. Over at Crossroads they're using these ideas. They're growing like crazy."

"So, you spent two days in Chicago by yourself."

"Yeah. That was kind of a drag, but it was worth it."

"I guess I don't understand why you took vacation time to go to a conference. I mean, we give you time for conferences and you have a budget for them, too. You've never used vacation time like that before."

"Oh, well, I did count those two, three days as conference time, not vacation time. I guess I really only used five days or so of actual vacation. You're right, I wouldn't use my days off to go to a conference. It's interesting and all, but it's still work."

"That makes sense. But there's still something a little weird about this vacation thing."

"What's that?"

"Well, you remember our conversation here before you left—the one when I asked you where you were going and you said Chicago."

"Yeah?"

"We were talking about family vacations—what we'd done with the kids, all the fun they'd had, and so on. I think I told you about taking Rachel to L.A., and then about going to D.C. to see all the monuments. You told me about taking your kids to Denver."

"You've got a good memory."

"Well, I love our vacations—put a lot of effort into them. So, anyway, only after we talked about all those things did I ask, 'Where are you going?'"

"Right."

"You answered Chicago."

"Right."

"I guess I could've said *y'all*. 'Where are y'all going?' Then maybe you would've said Fresno. That's probably what confused you. I said *you*. But I still don't understand, given that we'd been talking about family vacations, why you said Chicago and not Fresno, or why you didn't explain in more detail.

You might've said, 'Well, Amy and the kids are going to Fresno, and I'll take in a conference in Chicago and join them later.'"

"I must have been pretty out of it. Must've been past my bedtime, like it is now."

"Or why you kept talking about all the fun things for families to do in Chicago when you weren't taking your family there."

"Like I said, you've got a good memory. I sure don't remember all that."

"Yeah, well, these misunderstandings happen." I looked at him for a while, watched him rub his eyes and make tired gestures. "Say, it must've been expensive, going to Chicago and then flying all the way to Fresno."

"Well, yeah, but I do have that conference budget. By the time it was all said and done, it didn't cost that much more than if I'd gone with Amy and the kids to Fresno. It didn't hurt our family budget, anyway."

I looked at him some more.

He finally stretched his arms over his head and looked back at me. "I need to go home."

"Not just yet."

"What do you mean? It's late."

"Dave, after your Chicago trip, you never turned in receipts. You were never reimbursed for any expenses."

"I must've forgotten."

"That much money? No way. The trip must've been upward of two grand, with the conference fees and everything. You've never forgotten to turn in your receipts, because money in your household is tight. No. You were in Chicago, but not for a conference."

"What are you saying, Jim?"

"I'm saying you were in Chicago and Amy was in Fresno, when I thought you were both in Chicago. I'm saying I thought you two were together with the kids, because that's what you wanted me to think. I'm saying that you didn't want anyone to know you were in Chicago without Amy."

"Are you accusing me of lying to you?"

"I am."

"You're not going to consider that this may all be a misunderstanding? That you might not have seen the receipts? That I really might've forgotten this time? You're just going to call me a liar? After all we've been through tonight, talking heart-to-heart about my marriage, you're going to accuse me of lying about a trip I took last spring?"

"I am. You're lying to me about why you were in Chicago."

"Well, yeah, it looks like I am."

"It looks like you are because you are."

"I thought you were a gracious guy, Jim. I didn't think you of all people would look at appearances."

"What does graciousness have to do with it? A lie's a lie."

"I thought you had more mercy than to make a snap judgment about my integrity in the heat of the moment."

"A snap judgment?"

"You were different. I would expect this from the others."

"This is no snap—"

"But I was wrong—"

"I know the church's books like my own—"

"It turns out you're just like the rest of the old guard."

"It's no snap judgment for me to know you paid for that trip out of your own pocket."

"So my integrity's just a matter of dollars and cents with you."

Cue stomach. "No one else in this church would've sat with you all this time, listening to you, giving you the benefit of the doubt, trying to understand you."

"Some would have!"

"Who? The trustees?"

"Lots of people—people who haven't been in the poisonous atmosphere of this congregation for decades. New people."

"People who don't know you as well as I do."

"At least they would've tried to work it out. But you've just been waiting all this time for me to make a mistake. That's why you sat here with me."

"That's not true. I've been trying for two days to understand what you did and why. I've been trying to work it out."

"You were looking for evidence. You were fishing, like a prosecutor. This whole sabbatical thing was really about getting me fired after all."

"Dave!"

"What don't you like about me? Is it my T-shirts and Birks?"

"We've had our differences, but—"

"Is it my preaching?"

"No, I wasn't—"

"What would make you hunt for a reason to get me fired?"

"Dave, for Pete's sake!"

"Maybe you agree with your dad. Maybe you think I'm too dumb to run the church!"

I was silent for a time, feeling hot and sick. I massaged the back of my neck and looked at the trash can. Maybe he was right. I was bellowing, just like Dad; making verbal jabs, just like Dad. I even felt my chest push out and my chin pull back like Dad's used to.

From my memory played the tearful pleas I'd made as a boy, when I despaired of ever making Dad believe I was truthful. He'd seen me at the drugstore when I'd said I was going bowling. My story about the flat bike tire didn't make any sense, so I must've been covering something. Boyhood for me was spent trying to keep his fire-breathing to a minimum. I swore I'd never lord it over people, never suspect people, yet here I was.

And I could see Mom, neck straight, mouth set in its wince, turning away from me like she did from Dad—the meaning as unclear as ever, but no less emasculating.

Maybe I'd lost it. Somewhere I could've jumped to a conclusion that cast Dave in the wrong light. But where? The confrontation had twisted so many directions by now, there was no hope of retracing it.

I sighed slowly through my teeth. "All right. Let's start over. Why did you go to Chicago?"

Dave looked me in the eye. "You seriously want me to tell you after you've just accused me of lying?" He shook his head.

"You wanted a chance to explain. I'm giving it to you."

"Too late. You said you don't trust me. Feeling's mutual."

"We're not there anymore. We're way beyond personal trust. Now we're talking about your ministry. You want a chance to explain Chicago? You'd better take it."

He looked back at the table. "I needed to be alone."

"Be alone?"

"I wanted to get away by myself for a while."

"Why?"

"There are too many demands on me. I never get time for myself. I have to meet with all these people and absorb their emotions. I have to help them cope. I have to coordinate my leaders and make sure they don't irritate each other too much. Then I have to care for my family. And when I'm not doing those things, I'm studying for sermons and Sunday school talks and training sessions. I'm reading about controversies and trying to keep up with what everyone is talking about. I never get time for myself.

"You know, you guys say the job is forty hours a week, and you claim that I get two days off. But the reality is, there are no days off. If a crisis comes up on Saturday, I have to spend just as much time as I would on Tuesday. If people call the house and interrupt my evening at home, they have just as much right to my time as they would if they'd called the office at 9:30 in the morning. If I'm in town, I'm on call—no matter what day it is.

"I went to Chicago because I wanted to be alone, Jim. So now I get punished for that. Now I'm sneaking off without permission. I'm accused of lying about my comings and goings."

I heard my voice rise over the top of his. "No, Dave. That's not what's going on here. I don't care whether you take time for yourself, and I don't care whether you go to Chicago or Fresno or Tasmania to do it. I don't even care whether you take your family. Do whatever you want. But I care a great deal when you don't tell me the truth."

"That's exactly what I'm talking about. Accusations."

"First, you requested a week's vacation because you needed time with your family. Then, when you went, it turned out you wanted to go to this conference. But you never got reimbursed for it. So after that rationale's been challenged, you've come up with another one—time for yourself."

"Doesn't prove anything, except that you're determined to brand me a liar."

"No matter how I look at it, you lied to me about there being a conference. And if you lied about the conference, then

I think you also lied to me originally when you implied that your whole family was going with you. You slipped the lie through a loophole in a pronoun."

His hand fell on the table. "I don't believe this. Now we're on grammar!"

My voice now took on the pomposity of an AM radio talk-show host. "I'm left with this, Dave. I can't see why you would want to cover up taking personal time in Chicago. I can't see why it would be such a shameful thing that you'd first have to invent a family trip and then a Willow Creek conference to make sure I didn't find out about it. This latest rationale is another cover-up."

"So why did you even ask?"

More talk-show voice. "Before, of course, you were telling me things I couldn't verify. You told me about your motivations for talking to Kim, your reasons for taking the drive with her, your dissatisfactions with Amy—all of which I could believe or disbelieve, but none of which I could treat as established fact." I could hear how I sounded, but I couldn't stop. "But now we've arrived on different ground. I can test your statements. I can confirm or disprove your claims."

"Good for you."

"Do you think I should ask Amy what you told her about Chicago?"

Dave went white.

Now my elation was mixed with shame. I had cornered him, but in doing so I had trampled all my aspirations. I slumped.

His voice was pinched, narrow. "How about I just settle this whole thing and quit? Isn't that what you want?"

I glared and started to respond, but the voice I heard now was hoarse and tired. "What I want is gone. Believe it or not, Dave, I wanted to follow grace. It's been like my pillar of cloud.

I was hoping I could follow it out of the wasteland this church keeps wandering in. But I've lost that grace in the dark, Dave, and I don't know where to find it.

"I'm following the truth tonight and it's leading me where I never wanted to go—back over the old trails. I'm dwelling on your faults, trying to figure out what you've done. I'm suspecting everything you say and judging you for every little mistake. There isn't any other way to meet my responsibilities. Truth is rising and I have to follow it.

"And tomorrow I'll go even further: I will punish you. Your lying bears a price, and I will exact it. I don't know what the figure will be, and I'm not even sure how to run the moral numbers.

"This is not what I wanted. I can't seem to do any of it without getting angry—the very thing I swore I wouldn't do. I hate the way I sound. I'm just not an angry man. I like a little distance, some dispassionate oil to keep the voice sweet. But I can't finesse this one. I can't forget the humiliation of being tricked, no matter how gracious forgetting it would be. What would that grace be worth without truth? How can I forgive unless there's been a verified offense with a price tag on it? So anger it is.

"Like I said, I don't know what happened to my pillar of cloud—honestly, I don't. Maybe I hallucinated. I hope not. But I don't have a doctrine or a Bible verse to give me a quick answer. Tonight, I'll just try to get the big things right and sort out the contradictions later.

"And if that means I become what I hate—an enforcer with shame for a nightstick—then for the sake of ridding this church of your lies, that's what I'll do. Tell me what you did in Chicago!"

Dave began to cry.

14

Less than nineteen hours later, when I sat down with the trustees, there was the usual premeeting banter—Mike talking about yet more Democratic perfidy, Jake gossiping about developers, Dick teasing Eddy about his eating habits. But it was half-hearted. Tom's courtesy laughs at the one-liners gave the clearest evidence of an elephant in the room. They all knew we never met on Thursdays. They'd only heard about the meeting just before lunch, and I insisted they break any engagements to attend it. They probably thought I looked terrible—especially Earl, who made furtive glances at my swollen eyes and razor-burned cheeks.

So, for once, they didn't care about politics and land deals. In a weird inversion of accepted protocol, the banter became a formulaic ritual and the meeting was the real event.

Tom's token laughter ceased abruptly and his eyes panned the table. One by one, the other trustees cleared their throats and fell silent—Eddy got out his notebook, Dick folded his arms, then Earl looked up at the ceiling. Jake caught on last, his yarn about the builder north of town trailing off without a punch line.

I wondered who was the last Israelite to stop dancing and notice Moses on the ridge with the broken tablets of stone at his feet.

It did seem to me that Pastor Dave's dance had finally come to an end all those hours earlier. He seemed to have given up hope of concealment and it took him quite a while to regain his composure. He was prostrate, slumped on the tabletop with his head in his hands, his shoulders heaving. As I watched this, it struck me that men's crying looks like laughter.

Naturally, my only question was how bad his admissions were going to be—how long the affair had gone on, how much he'd lied. Dave's relationship with Kim was all I had in my sights—and that by his design. I was still thinking in the sequence of his choosing, from A to B to C, in that order, with no interruptions or impertinent questions. That sequence, in which I was guided from one admission to the next—only on a need-to-know basis—was Dave's strongest defense. So there I was, patiently waiting for him to have his cry so that I could hear what I knew was coming.

"I lied to you, Jim."

"I know that. What have you lied about?"

"I lied about yesterday afternoon. I told you that I'd talked to Kim for the first time in many years as if it happened yesterday."

"It didn't happen?"

"It didn't happen yesterday. It all happened pretty much the way I described, but last February."

"Last February!" It's one thing to know in the abstract that someone has lied. But it's another to itemize the betrayal. He told me an incident from last February? As if it'd happened yesterday? How could he conceive of doing such a thing? How could he have pretended all evening that the ride I'd seen had been his first ride with Kim? How could he have voluntarily confessed all his failings as if they'd happened yesterday when he knew they'd happened months ago? How could he so abuse my faith? "You'd better spill this whole thing right now."

His shoulders shot up. "Everything I told you was true, except that it happened in February. We met exactly the way I described, and we talked for the reasons I described. We took the drive over to the church, just the way I said. I didn't mean for it to go any further than that."

His shoulders slowly relaxed. "But we had more talks at the Bean over the next month or so. We crossed paths in our daily routines. We didn't change anything or alter our schedules to meet—we didn't have to. We knew we would meet. At first, it happened a couple times a week. We'd talk for fifteen minutes or a half-hour—however much time we had. But soon we were meeting every day, almost like a standing appointment."

No wonder those two Bean employees had been so interested to see Dave get out of Kim's car. No wonder they grinned at each other. Dave and Kim had been an item for a long time. "Then what?"

"I began to love her."

No, Jim, I thought, *it would not be appropriate right now to point out that this development was completely predictable. Keep your sarcasm to yourself. Keep your trap shut.*

"She's attractive, of course. So much more than in high school. She's so skilled in everything she does. So orderly and methodical. She works in real estate and has a lot of responsibility at the office. She's so fluent and sociable, easy with people, outgoing. And I guess she was sympathetic to me in all the frustrations I was having. She'd listen to me describe things that were going on at church and she'd always have helpful suggestions. She'd listen to my marriage frustrations. I needed someone to talk to, I guess."

"So you've been having an affair." *Don't get mad again. You know what'll happen if you get mad again.*

"Jim, we're in love. I didn't plan it that way. I didn't go looking for it. I didn't even want it. But it happened. The more we talked, the more I felt I could share. I felt safe with Kim, like I could tell her anything and she would understand. I wanted that kind of intimacy."

No, Jim, no! Shut your trap! "Dave, that is not intimacy." *Idiot!*

"What are you talking about? When someone receives you as a real person with needs, and responds to you honestly, and doesn't suspect you all the time—that isn't intimacy?"

Rabbit trail, idiot! You'll never get back on course if you reply to that. "No, it's not intimacy. The people we're truly intimate with suspect us all the time because they know us." *Oh, that's good, Jim. Always finding your eloquence in exaggeration. See what the master strategist does with that one.* "We can't fool the people who love us. They've seen our patterns too often and they've heard every excuse. Our true intimates aren't persuaded by our words anymore. They watch to see whether our patterns change. What you're talking about is not a person you can be intimate with. You're talking about a person you can buffalo with sympathy ploys and guilt trips. You're talking about a woman who's trying to be polite when she listens to you—maybe for her own selfish reasons—and who won't press you too hard on specifics."

"That's a great, middle-class American version of intimacy, Jim. *Suspicion.* I'm talking about a higher level of acceptance."

See there? Never open yourself up for a cheap shot with this guy! Idiot!
"Higher level of acceptance! You're talking about a *betrayal* of intimacy, that's what you're talking about. A flight from accountability. You found a new relationship with a woman who doesn't know you as well as Amy does, and you liked the freedom she gave you to reinterpret yourself. You had intimacy, Dave. You had it with Amy. You threw that intimacy away so you could have this affair."

"I can't believe you're seriously telling me that intimacy is all about suspicion. You can't have intimacy without trust. I have trust with Kim in a way I've never had it with Amy. Like I say, I can tell Kim anything and she won't judge or criticize or condemn."

"Of course you can tell her anything. She's never heard it before. But see how long this trust between you lasts when she starts hearing it all again. And again, and again. What's your trust founded on? Nothing but ignorance. She hasn't found the skips in your record yet."

"So intimacy is when you know exactly what your spouse is going to say and you roll your eyes before she says it? Nice."

Try listening next time, Jim. You wouldn't be in this argument if you'd listened. "No. Intimacy is both of you knowing what the other's going to say, knowing you're not going to buy it, but persevering anyway. You don't clam up. You keep talking, exposing your follies to the other, and looking for the way forward."

"We're not going to agree on this."

"Not if you're trying to justify an affair on such flimsy grounds. Let me ask you something: Is Kim married? Does she have kids?"

"Yes. One boy."

"Who do you think knows her better? Her husband, or you? Her husband, who's heard every excuse before, every complaint, every lie—or you, who are hearing it all for the first time?"

"Intimacy is about acceptance, not knowledge or ignorance."

"You won't answer me because you know that your understanding of Kim is nothing compared to her husband's. She's betraying intimacy just like you. She's throwing it away for the freedom you're giving her."

"Like I say, we're not going to agree on this."

"You two have made a contract that you'll give one another freedom as long as you both shall love."

"You're twisting this, Jim. You're angry with me, and I can understand that, but you're still twisting my words. If you think intimacy is about holding the past over one another's heads like a club and beating one another into submission with it, then you don't understand what relationships are about. For that matter, you don't understand what the gospel is about. The gospel isn't about suspicion. It's about acceptance. It's about frail, needy, broken people accepting each other and living with each other's woundedness."

"Don't talk to me about the gospel! If it's one thing I'm not prepared to sit for right now it's your hyperspiritual phrases! You're having an affair! That disqualifies you from teaching me anything about 'higher levels' of anything, especially the gospel. In your mouth, it all turns into a soupy mess, and it's too rich for me. Way too rich!"

"I don't think of myself as betraying the gospel, Jim. I still think that, in my own way, I'm living the gospel."

I waved both hands. "Whatever. You can think what you want to think. But you still haven't told me what actually happened when I saw you. All I know is what you did last February. What were you doing yesterday afternoon?"

Dave sighed. "Kim and I had gone to lunch. Out of town."

I struggled to breathe, my stomach churning again. "You pretended you'd had an innocuous little reunion when you were really off romancing this woman? You fed me all those fake complaints to cover up your affair, maybe even lay the groundwork to justify it."

Dave was crying again. "No! The stuff I told you about Amy was true. I really am frustrated. I didn't make any of that up. It wasn't fake!"

"So what? So what if it was true? So what if it was ten times worse than you said? It wouldn't change the fact that you fed it all to me to get me off the subject—to deceive me. It was cold-blooded betrayal. You waved at me from the Bean like nothing was amiss. At your house, you asked me whether I had come over to ask about your being dropped off by Kim. You brought it up in order to take control of the conversation! You revealed all your indiscretions, apparently of your own free will—but it was all nauseating forthrightness designed to conceal. You have to understand, Dave, I don't care anymore about your disappointment in your marriage. Even if it's real, you used it to lie!"

"I admitted that I lied! I confessed it!"

"Yes, but you're still pleading for the true parts of your story. You think I should forgive your lies because parts of what you said were true. That doesn't wash. You didn't just lie about when the reunion happened. You didn't just deceive me about the calendar. You used the truth to lie. You covered up your sin with facts. You have me so confused that I can't tell a fact from a lie anymore. That's not just deception. That's some kind of demonic hypocrisy!"

Dave bounded up from his chair and hit the wall with his fist. He paced like a wolf. Now his voice rasped with anger.

"I am not a hypocrite. I saw enough hypocrisy growing up. I swore I'd never do what my parents did, trying to act pious and strong when they were really broken and needy; trying to keep up a front of religiosity when on the inside they had no life. No. I am not a hypocrite. At the very least I can claim that. I've worked my whole life to achieve this. And I won't let you mock me as if I've failed!"

I gawked like an onlooker at an auction, because he really wasn't talking to me. Dave's sudden passion cooled some of my wrath. Hypocrisy? His parents? This was too impulsive to be another trick.

I pushed back one more time. "What are you talking about? You preached on sexual purity. Now you're having an affair. You're saying one thing and doing another—a hypocrite. Open and shut."

"You haven't paid any attention to my sermons."

"Are you kidding? I sure paid attention when Rachel committed herself to purity after one of them. I heard that one loud and clear. What's she supposed to think now?"

"Like I said, if you think I've been preaching some kind of legalistic churchianity, where keeping the rules is all that matters, you haven't been paying any attention. Sexual purity is good, yes. It's God's will, yes. Kids should try to keep that ideal. They should be called to it. Purity should be held up for them as God's very best, like any other ideal of holiness. But that's not the core of the gospel, and I've never said it was."

I folded my hands.

Dave was still standing, half turned toward me but looking at the far wall. "This is a fallen world. It's full of the disease called sin, and we're all infected with it. Things don't always work out for God's best. We get hurt. We believe in people and they fail us. We love them and they don't love us back. Those kinds of hurts leave us needy, self-focused, prone to take from others more than we give. So this world has all these infected people wandering around, spreading the disease. Preachers can't hold up God's best in a sick world like this and say, 'I know you're all feeling pretty bad about your lives, but the main thing is to keep the rules.'

"The rules can only tell us what's healthiest. They're boundary lines that say, 'On this side is health, and on the other side is sickness.' There's no life or vitality in the rules. In fact, they're a kind of death. The whole world is on the sick side of the line. And if we do nothing but preach the boundaries, people will only hear, 'You're sick, you're sick.' Instead, we should only point to the boundary lines as a way of saying, 'The best life is over there. Let's get as close to it as we can.'

"That's what I was saying to the youth that Sunday when I talked about sexual purity—be healthy and get close to what God says is best. I wasn't saying, 'Keep the rules, or else you're a bad Christian.' I was just pointing them to the healthiest life before they got infected with sexual impurity and had to live with the consequences. The youth need to make good decisions, that's all.

"But many of them haven't and won't. Many of them, by the time I preached that sermon, had already become infected, were already needy and broken. The thing for them to do is admit their sickness and try to get well.

"That's really the whole point, Jim. I don't know any bad Christians. I only know sick people who are trying to get well.

"I'm sick with sin. I've never pretended otherwise. Sometimes the illness gets worse. That's not hypocrisy—not if you admit the illness. The hypocrite is a sick person who pretends to be healthy. And then, I just feel bad for him, because he doesn't have a chance of getting well until he admits he's sick."

He paused a moment and sat down, his hand draped over the back of an adjacent chair. The knuckles were scraped and oozed blood from where he had struck the wall.

"Remember when we found out Greg had that mistress? Remember how I dealt with it? Did I come down on him with condemnation? Did I put a bunch of rules on him? No. I just said, 'Greg, sin's getting the better of you here. You need to admit you've got this disease and start pursuing health again.' I said, 'Maybe we can talk about how you got infected in the first place. Let's talk about your disappointments, your hurts. Let's start moving you toward health.' He admitted his illness. Remember? You were there. He admitted it. He didn't want to do anything about it then, but there's still hope for him. He's not a hypocrite. And neither am I."

Sickness. Infection. Health. I had indeed heard those words in Dave's preaching. They were standard terms. But he was right; I hadn't paid attention. God's will was full of benefits, not mandates. Sin was unhealthy—bad for you—not necessarily wrong. And in confronting Greg, Dave never went so far as to use words like *wrong* or *evil*. He never talked in terms of betrayal, not even after Greg divorced his wife and left. Dave designed his gospel for people who lived in the ruin of divorce, addiction, and immorality, and who had to get along with those who had created the ruin.

How had I mistaken this man's teaching? Why had I heard *evil* when he meant *infected*? Why had I assumed firm standards where he only intended squishy ideals?

"I have one question, Dave. This system of yours, this version of sin as a disease—does this mean that the only true sin is thinking you're well?"

His red eyes shined with teacherly approval. "That's right. That's the only hypocrisy, the only dishonesty. Everything else is curable."

I glanced at the blood clots forming on his knuckles. "What about the destructiveness of sin? Don't you believe in evil? Isn't anything just *wrong*?"

"Well, Jim, I guess it's all wrong. It's all destructive. But we all participate in the destruction, so we can't judge each other. All we can do is forgive and strive for the ideal."

"So no one can judge your affair."

"I never had an affair."

15

I looked up from his hand and was met by a smile. I could almost ignore his swollen eyes; his good puppy look was back. The smile gave no hint that he'd been clinging to his job for the past five hours. He was finally telling the truth—leaning back, opening his hands, and giving his testimony.

He might've been in the pulpit.

But the more I heard, the more I wished Pastor Dave had kept lying. At least that way his sincerity wouldn't have condemned him. He shifted in his chair and leaned over the table, his face craning toward me as if to kiss my cheek, the very incarnation of grace.

"You keep calling it an affair, Jim, but that's not what it was—or is. I guess a lot of adultery is frivolous—maybe most of it is. An affair is a shallow, physical attraction. Playing around. But not every situation is that way. Sometimes it grows out of something larger, and that's the way it was with Kim and me."

He leaned back again. "Sometimes you find life in a video store. The summer before my senior year in high school, I went to Bob's Video practically every night for the air-conditioning. I'd pace the aisles, waiting for one of the boxes to grab me, and after my eyes glazed I'd snag an action flick and get in line. That's where I first saw Kim. One night she was the new girl at the register.

"She absolutely beamed. Every customer got a smile loud enough to mute the overhead music. Her eyes reached out. Her 'Hi!' almost gave you a hug, and each one was pitched differently, like she had an X-ray of each customer's personality. She guided people through the checkout with the assurance of a five-star maître d'.

"Her face hypnotized me. It was a strong, ethnic face—dark eyes, olive complexion, Roman nose, a wide mouth out of proportion with everything else—all surrounded by wayward black hair. Her face was full of tricks and flashes, symmetrical enough to catch your eye, but thrown a little bit off balance. One eye squinted tighter than the other when she smiled, and the crinkles on one side wandered upward while on the other side they wandered down. It even seemed like her mouth was off-center, like it moved independent of the rest of her face.

"When I got up to the counter, she started talking to me as if she'd known me her whole life. I couldn't do anything but smile and nod. It turned out she had just moved into town with her mom and they lived just a few blocks on the other side of Calder Avenue. She was going to be a sophomore at Central.

"Then she finished ringing me up, handed me my change, and I walked out the door. I was blocks away on my bike before I realized how abruptly she'd sent me off. But it didn't matter. All I could think about was her right eye shining at me over her shoulder when she turned."

Listening to Dave in his reverie, I couldn't keep my shoulders from rising. I also couldn't keep from hating this woman I'd never met.

Dave chuckled. "I rode around for an hour, replaying everything she'd said. You know the neighborhood. No sidewalks. The houses all sagged. It was all overgrown bushes and dirty cars, but for once the place didn't fill me with contempt. If I could get a dose of her smile every day, the junk that filled my life just might be bearable.

"At least that's how I felt until I got back to the house. You ever see Mom's place?"

I shook my head.

"Our lamppost disappeared into a bougainvillea. The weeds on our lawn that weren't dead were two feet high, and the only way to tell them apart from the weeds in the flower beds was by the railroad ties that used to make a border—if you could find them. I doubt our gutters were ever cleaned. Mom's Pinto looked like it'd survived a thermonuclear blast. And the final touch was the old freezer stowed under a crape myrtle along the side of the house.

"Steering my bike around the oil stains on the driveway that night made me feel like white trash. I yanked the garage door open, wondering whether the handle would pull free of the plywood again. After years in the sun, the paint had curled and receded like a bad head of hair. But that wasn't the worst. The worst was the smell of mildew and never-replaced kitty litter that stunned me when the door rose. I held my breath and jammed my bike between the stack of boxes full of canning supplies and the dusty couch we had looted from Grandma's house after she died. As quick as I could, I pulled on the rope to slam the door back down, and then I could breathe again.

"Mom didn't even say hi when I came in the front door. She was leaning over some Chinese takeout or something, trying to charm her latest guy.

"When a guy was in the house, I didn't exist. I'd walk in and Mom would be leaning forward just far enough, smiling just coy enough, and laughing just loud enough to keep the guy's attention. Her hair was always extra fluffy when these guys came to the house, and her blouse would have just the right voltage of tease. What caliber of guy was there depended on whether Mom was working—and where. She was at the library that summer—at least for a month—and this latest guy had been framing houses across the street. She'd hooked him by parking two straight days in front of the house he was building, and grinning at him before she sashayed across the street to work. I know because I was there. I'd get my bike out of the trunk and ride away, trying not to watch her.

"It turned out Library Guy used speed like I use coffee, so he'd sit in our mold-perfumed kitchen in a daze, wiping sweat off his oily face and rubbing his nose. Whenever I came home, I'd cut from the front door, around the bean bag chairs on the family room floor, to the hallway before the guy could flash me his victory grin. My room was where I'd stay the rest of the night.

"It was pretty nice, actually. I kept it painted and clean, and I kept air fresheners going to cover the cat smell. Plus I had media. When I went to Dad's for the weekend, he'd have another stereo component or speaker or TV for me to take home. He made sure I had a Mac and a Walkman. I even had a fridge. I could tune most things out if I needed to.

"But I couldn't tune out everything. I still needed actual food. I still had to go to the bathroom. So I developed strategies.

If I heard Mom's muffled laughter, I knew they were probably making out in front of a movie. I'd ease my door open, slide along the wood floor, and duck into the kitchen without glancing toward the family room, hoping they stayed busy and didn't notice me.

"The bathroom was less problematic, since it was right across the hall. But even getting in there was sometimes a challenge. One night I had to go really bad, but I could hear Library Guy pacing the house and breathing like he'd just run a marathon. Then I heard a heavy slap. I peered out and saw the guy sprawled naked on the bathroom tile. I looked in Mom's room and she was snoozing away. So I pulled on some shorts, rode to the AM-PM and used the bathroom there."

Dave's steady tone seemed disconnected to what he was saying. I'd never had a glimpse into his life with his mom. Now my shoulders slumped.

"The night I first saw Kim was typical. I cut across the family room to the hall, watched a movie in my room, and played some video games. Then I got seriously hungry. I waited until I heard Mom's laughter, and then I slid down the hall into the kitchen, and unwrapped a burrito.

"Then my mom came in. She said, 'I don't think it's good for you to be locked in your room all the time.'

"I didn't say anything. Just put the burrito in the microwave and fired it up. Then Mom says—and again, this was typical—'I've got some bad news. The library hasn't worked out. Today was my last day. I guess we'll have to make the clothes you've got work for school—at least for the fall.' Which of course meant *I* would have to make them work.

"I got a job the next day, mowing lawns. I put in as many hours as I could during the summer, and I found other work after school started. I bought my own clothes. I even bought a car and paid the insurance. I wasn't going to be a prisoner to Mom's laziness."

I nodded my head to show I'd heard him, but then I said, "We're off track, Dave. Let's get back to Kim."

He winced and looked away. "I wasn't off track, but . . . whatever. Every day I made sure to get to Bob's before her shift ended. Her energy was amazing. She worked as fast when the line had two people as when it had fifteen. When she finished ringing people up, she closed the register drawer like it was a trampoline launching her to help more customers, or clean windows, or put up new posters.

"I always lingered until the line was short. I knew I wasn't presentable after a day of mowing, but I couldn't stay away. If I did it right, I was the last in line and the store was empty.

"One night—it was the last week of summer—her neon got brighter when I came to the register. She looked behind her and then back at me. 'I'm off in about fifteen minutes,' she said. 'Wanna hang out?'

"We walked to her house a couple blocks away, and she never stayed in the same posture for more than three seconds. Her jazzy gait made her shoulders dip in syncopated rhythms, and her arms swung uncoordinated because she didn't have anything to carry. I snapped glances at her when she looked away, almost checking to be sure she was really there.

"She lived in a neighborhood just like where Mom and I lived. Same junky places and filthy cars. But in the middle of all the rundown shacks, under an elm on one side and an ash on the other, was a 1950s tract house, same as Mom's. The light was still strong enough to see it was pristine. The lawn was mostly weeds rather than grass, but it was green and mowed.

The beds next to the lawn's sharp edges had close-clipped jasmine and geraniums, the dirt turned over and not a weed in sight. The house hadn't been painted in years, but everything was tidy.

"There was a lady on her knees near one of the flower beds, digging out a weed. To my surprise, Kim called, 'Hey, Mom, I want you to meet my friend Dave. He goes to Central.'

"Her mom stood up and took off her gloves and extended her hand to me. She invited me inside for something to drink, but Kim said she was starving, and the next thing I knew I was staying for dinner.

"We had a nice conversation over dinner, talking about all the places they had traveled when Kim's mom was still married to her dad. They'd been to France and Germany, Ireland, Mexico, and even New Zealand, and they had some great stories.

"After dinner was over, Kim's mom disappeared into another part of the house, and we finished the dishes. Then we went into Kim's bedroom, and she shut the door. She turned on George Michael and plopped on the bed, while I sat down backward on the desk chair, straddling the back.

"I'd never been in a girl's room before. The fragrance of creams and perfumes was new. She had posters of Wham! and The Police, but what really caught my eye was the sense of everything being finished; there was no corner left bare and unsoftened. I realized I didn't know what completeness was.

"She was talking about all her coworkers and customers at Bob's, but I didn't hear much. I just looked at her and marveled.

"She lay on her stomach with her feet bouncing behind her. We talked about why our parents had split up and she told me about how hard it had been to move to our town, and how unfriendly everyone was. Everyone but me.

"And then she kind of rolled onto her side and looked at me with an arched eyebrow. I didn't need any other hints."

16

Dave let his revelation sink in. I cringed, shifting in my seat. "So how long did you two carry on in high school?"

He was waiting for that one. "After school started, I hardly saw her. You know how big Central was. I looked for her all day on the first day of school with no luck. We didn't have any classes together, and I didn't pass her in the halls. I sat on the brick sign out front all through lunch watching for her, but she never passed by.

"And then, after school, I had to get to my job, so I couldn't wait around. I only found her later that evening, at Bob's. The store was jammed, and she lit up when I got to the front of the line, but she didn't have time to talk. I asked if she was free after work, but she already had homework. I said, 'Maybe I'll see you tomorrow,' and she said, 'I hope so!' but the next day was the same. In fact, weeks passed like this.

"I was working a lot, trying to save money for college, and it seemed like she went out of town a lot on weekends, either visiting her dad or pet-sitting for some friend of her mom's, so between school and work and who knows what, we rarely saw each other.

"And then, one day at school, I found her. She was sitting alone during lunch on what students called The Quad—a large square of weed-infested lawn at the center of campus. She was eating salad from a plastic carton. Her shoulders were raised and her elbows drawn in. She was focused on the salad, occasionally flashing sidelong glances at a group of cheerleaders sitting on the grass nearby. When she saw me, the neon switched on and she waved, so I went over. We had a nice conversation, and she looked at me like she had in her room that first night. She loved me, Jim. She wanted to be with me, I know it."

Dave was leaning toward me like he was going to seize my shoulders. I held up a hand. "Okay. I just don't see what any of this has to do with your adultery."

"I'm getting to that."

"You said your adultery grew out of something larger than lust. I'm not seeing it."

"I said I'm getting to that." Dave sat back with a sigh. "I'm just trying to tell you I couldn't understand why our relationship never went anywhere. Obviously, you don't get it."

"Oh, I get that you two had a little fling in high school, but I don't see how that sanctifies your adultery. How about we just skip forward to that part."

Dave went back to picking at the veneer on the edge of the table. "Kim tried to reach out later—a couple of times. The last week of school, she tracked me down to write in my yearbook. Made a big deal about it, and when she was done, she said, 'You can't read this now or I'll be embarrassed.'

"Her note was no big deal—it said, 'Dave, you've been a good friend to me. I know you'll have an awesome life! You're the greatest!'—but she put so much importance on it. And then, I didn't see her again until last February."

"Okay, Dave, but I'm still not seeing what this has to do with—"

"She reached out one more time. Even though I never told her where I was going to college, nearly two years later, she found out. She wrote me a letter that I still have. Superficially, she was asking about my school. Did I like it? How were the professors? Did I pledge? But there was one sentence in the middle of all the questions—one was all she needed—that told me she still loved me. 'I'm attracted to the school, but you're a big draw too.'

"I didn't know how to respond. I had come to Christ by that time. I was seriously dating Amy. I didn't want Kim to show up, because I knew she would eclipse everything else. I wrote back, but buried a reference to Amy in all the catch-up news. That seemed to work, because she never wrote back or visited the school.

"But the letter left me with unanswered questions. Why did Kim never pursue our relationship? Sometimes, even after Amy and I were married, I'd pull out the letter just to read that one sentence."

"So last February you saw her."

"Yeah. When we recognized each other that day at the Bean, she lit up, just like she used to do twenty years ago. We chatted for a few minutes, and after the usual questions, she glanced at all the notes I had on the table and asked what I was working on. When I told her it was my sermon for Sunday morning, she froze.

"Then she says, 'What did you say?'

"I said, 'I'm the pastor over at the Baptist church.'

"And she said, 'That's ... unexpected. I mean, it's great, but ... what made you do that? I mean, why'd you choose that?'

"We sat down at the table and I gave her my testimony—how I got very good at making money but found it didn't give me any freedom. I told her how I had partied when I was off work and didn't get any freedom from that, either. I said, 'When I found Jesus, I realized how liberating it was to admit I was wounded—by my parents, by my own decisions. I couldn't live life on my own and I didn't have to.'

"The next day, Kim met me at the Bean again. We chatted awhile and she told me about her life. Her husband is a vascular surgeon. Top of his class, top of his specialty, top of the list of donors at any nonprofit you want to name. She doesn't have to work, but she likes to have her own money and doesn't want to just sit around, so she opened a real estate office when her son started junior high—he's in high school now—and she's been pretty successful at it. Over the years, she and her husband just kind of drifted apart—he puts in eighty-hour weeks—and they reached a point where they were barely seeing each other anymore.

"She seemed interested in what I was doing, and I invited her to come to church, but she has no religious background at all and said she'd feel uncomfortable. So, a week later, we started a Bible study right there at the Bean. Every day, we talked about some aspect of our brokenness. I've never been so passionate about praying for a person in my whole life as I was about praying for Kim.

"I finally showed her the most important verse in the Bible, my personal favorite: 'I came that you might have life, and have it abundantly.' When she read it out loud, a tear started to slide down her cheek. She tried to whisk it away, but it kept coming. Finally, she smiled and said, 'Okay, I'm wounded too. But these words help—really. You're making me feel free again.'

"And then she looked at me."

Dave paused and stared at his hands. "We went—"

"I think I've heard enough."

"Honestly, Jim, I didn't start out to rekindle something with Kim."

"You've told me enough."

"If someone had shown me where we'd end up, I wouldn't have witnessed to her at all. But I didn't see that far ahead. I was too focused on her needs."

"You were focused on yourself."

"No—"

"You were obsessed."

"I can see now I've made a real mess. I've committed adultery. But you have to understand—"

"I do understand."

"No you don't. Whatever else it may be, my relationship with Kim is not an affair. There's nothing frivolous about it. It's not based on physical desire. It's based on giving. Our physical attraction came from the sharing."

"It doesn't—"

"I've given her my whole being. I've given Kim my heart because she meets my needs and I meet hers."

"I don't care—"

"Is that on the unhealthy side of the boundaries? Yes. Do I need to admit all the brokenness that led to this and find my way back to health? Yes. Do I need Jesus to heal me again? More than ever."

I worked my jaw in silence.

Dave kept filibustering. "But the question is, how do I move on from this? I'm not going to focus on condemnation. I'm going to pursue health and life with Jesus. I can't keep going this way, with two women in my life. Maybe the way back to health is to break off the relationship with Kim and renew my devotion to Amy. But leaving Amy may also be the way back. It may be that my marriage is the unhealthy relationship. I don't know which way to go—but I know God can work through this. Even though I've gotten so far out of his will, he can take this situation and create good in it. It's already happening. You've forced these issues into the open, Jim. Now we can all be honest about them. I can be honest with my kids and not pretend everything's okay when it isn't. I can be honest with Amy. I can be honest with the church. It's going to be hurtful, but sincerity is God's instrument."

My throat felt constricted. My mind replayed the yelling and squealing coming from Dave's house earlier that evening. The picture of Derek and Amanda hanging from their daddy froze in my memory. That would be their final playtime— maybe the last minutes of stress-free happiness they'd have. This wasn't just going to be hurtful for them; it was going to be catastrophic.

I asked the most neutral question I could think of. "Did you get your questions answered?"

"What questions?"

"About high school and that letter she wrote. Did she ever tell you what happened?"

"Oh, those questions." Dave was wallowing in all the healing he was about to experience at everyone else's expense, and oblivious to my clenched fist on the table. "You know, it's funny. I finally asked her about the letter, but she didn't remember writing it. She said, 'I wrote to you at college?! Weird! I don't remember that at all.' But by that point in our relationship, my questions didn't matter so much."

My knuckles were white. "You're telling me the things that preoccupied you for years she didn't even remember?"

"Well, I wouldn't say I was preoccupied, necessarily, but yeah."

"But you did say you were preoccupied. You said the unanswered questions bothered you. You said you kept reading her letter, even after you were married to Amy."

"Well, all my questions were answered. She pursued me. That was all I needed to know."

I shook my head and pressed my fist hard into the table. "That letter meant *nothing* to her. You were obsessed with trivialities."

"Our relationship in high school was not trivial—"

I held up my other hand and leaned across the table. "Dave, what is your rationale for this relationship?"

"Rationale?"

"Your stated reason for pursuing a new relationship with Kim was to resolve questions. Now here you are in adultery with her, and your questions were non-issues. What you had built up as a mystery about your past was just a fantasy. And for a fantasy, you've destroyed your marriage."

Dave stared at my finger in his face. "I don't see it that way. It was sort of funny that Kim didn't remember the letter. Sort of ironic. But by the time I realized that, we were way too far into the relationship."

"So what is this new relationship based on?"

"Kim just wanted to pursue it this time. I guess that's what it boils down to. I honestly think she was at a point of need that she didn't have before."

"So this relationship is founded on need."

"Right. That's what I've been saying."

"Aren't needs temporary? Don't they change?"

"Sure they do. People grow and develop."

"Dave, your marriage with Amy is founded on an oath. This thing with Kim is founded on needs. How can you think of the two as alternatives?"

Dave sneered. "What do you mean my marriage is founded on an oath? The ceremony was never the foundation of our marriage."

Both my hands were now clenched, and I shook them in front of his face. "The oath! Your marriage is founded on the oath you made!"

"Whatever. Ceremony, oath. My marriage with Amy was founded on needs, just like every other human relationship. In God's best plan, our needs are met in marriage. That's the way it's supposed to work. But in this fallen world, it usually doesn't work out that way."

My jaw hung like a broken branch. "So you don't view the oath you took as something binding."

"Well, it should be, I guess. But sometimes you just have to move on."

"Do you admit that breaking your oath is wrong?"

Dave looked at me in wonder. "The whole world is wrong, Jim."

I sat back and took in his amazement, replaying the astonished tone in his voice. This was what I'd been looking for. "So you're saying everything is so messed up that pointing out a wrong here or there doesn't help. It's all wrong, everything we do, and no single action is any more or less wrong than another."

"Exactly. All have sinned and fall short of the glory of God."

"So we just admit to God that we have a problem."

"He just wants sincerity. That's right."

I slumped back down in my chair.

Dave's preaching and leadership had indeed been consistent with his conduct. For seven years he had preached sin as "unhealthy behavior." In that time, he had never lowered the boom on anyone for any particular fault, but had urged us all to get as close to God's best as we could. Now that he was caught in adultery, he expected to get the same measure he had given. He expected understanding and forgiveness. Just as he had condemned no one, he expected no one would condemn him.

Wasn't that what the gospel was all about?

17

As I look back on how I reported to the trustees, I would do a lot of things differently if I were doing it today.

At the time, I relayed facts without injecting commentary. Here's what I saw; here's what I heard. I thought the facts would speak for themselves. The trustees would hear the contradictions, the lies, the rationalizations, and then tell the congregation the pastor was fired—it was all so obvious. It seemed to me that editorializing about Dave would be unfair somehow.

But I forgot how little the bare facts had affected me.

At least three times over the past two days, I'd thought the problem was solved. Dave wasn't really the guy in the Mercedes. Dave wouldn't reveal so much if he were lying. Dave would take a sabbatical. And all the solutions seemed reasonable at the time.

I only delved further after each of those pauses because something forced me to. Dave waved at me from the Bean. Audrey suggested the possibility that Dave had lied. I remembered a casual chat about family vacations.

In none of those moments did the facts change. Only my perspective.

The trustees were in no better position to interpret Dave's behavior. In fact, their perspective was even worse than mine. They needed more than reporting to understand him. They needed more than any editorializing I could've done. They needed a new religion.

And I only had indignation to offer, like Moses complaining that the Israelites had rejected him yet again. Maybe if I'd been better armed with the gospel—if I had portrayed Dave's sins as black marks against Christ's name—things would have turned out differently. Maybe the trustees would've seen the need to teach the congregation about holiness. Maybe the trustees would've learned about holiness themselves.

Maybe. But I was up against some long-standing precedents.

So they'd listened to my report like men on trial—Eddy taking notes, Mike fidgeting, Jake staring at the table, Earl staring at the ceiling, Dick contemplating the gut on which he rested his folded arms. Only Tom had returned my gaze with a look of sympathetic indignation.

The previous evening, around midnight, when Dave finally ended his story, I was looking for a way out of the mess. I had shed my old perceptions of Dave's preaching, sin, the church's history, grace itself. How was I to understand his adultery? Not on Dave's terms but my own. What were my terms? One confrontation wasn't enough to get closure.

"Dave, I'm going home to think. I don't know what to do about this. Something has to be done, but I have no idea what it is. So I'm going to reflect, and probably consult with some people. Don't come into the office tomorrow. Spend the day with your family."

He was tearful again. He said nothing, but merely walked out, got in his car, and drove away.

I entered the familiar darkness of my home. I never turned the lights on when I came in late because I didn't need them. Light or no light, I had mastered the house—where the door-knobs were, the sharp corners in the cabinetry, and where Rachel left her stuff. I hung my coat on the hook that was two-and-a-half paces to the right of the door from the garage. I strode through the kitchen, pausing by Rachel's door on the off chance she would still be awake. She wasn't. I slipped my hand around the doorknob to the master bedroom and padded in.

Audrey's form was buried under the blankets, outlined by a bit of moonlight slipping through the blinds. She didn't move, but I knew she was awake. As I shed my crumpled, stale clothes and nudged them toward the hamper, she spoke.

"Is he having an affair?"

"That depends."

"Great! Our pastor's Bill Clinton."

She'd been working on that one a while. "Let's talk about it in the morning. I need to get some sleep."

That wasn't going to happen. I had a sick stomach and a whirling mind. Fragments of the evening recurred and various speeches I might have made auditioned too late in my groggy imagination. It's possible I dreamt much of it.

After a few hours of this—and several trips to the bath-room—I was completely awake, as geared up as if it were seven o'clock on any ordinary morning. There was nothing else to do but think.

I lay on my back, searching my mind for some sort of frame for all these problems, some large issue that would encompass the others. Was this about adultery? Sure it was, but there were so many more issues. The adultery seemed like only a small part of it. Was it about lying? Definitely. Whatever sins a man commits, there is a measure of healing when he tells the truth. But Dave had lied to me so deliberately, and had calibrated his lies so carefully to my tendencies, that his admissions of the truth only fueled my rage.

The problem with Dave was that he'd arranged his life so that adultery and deceit could not be called hypocrisy. He'd written escape clauses into the gospel contract he preached, so that when he cheated on his wife and lied about it, he couldn't be found in breach. More than that, he even thought his acts fulfilled the terms.

Was my pastor even a Christian?

There was another problem: no one had noticed Dave's religion, whatever it was. Somehow his seminary professors had passed over it, even though doctrine is their area of expertise. The church where he was youth pastor missed it too. Our search committee hadn't noticed it. And neither had I. I'd paid close attention through decades of preaching by other pastors—good preaching, I thought—yet I'd listened to Dave for seven years without the slightest discomfort. I'd mistaken his new content for a different style.

"Want something to eat, sleepyhead?"

"Yeah, I guess so."

Audrey and I shuffled through the dark to the kitchen, permitting ourselves a brief look at our daughter, who was profoundly asleep in the glow of her screen saver. We always loved to watch her sleep. It made all seem right with the world.

Audrey flicked on one of the kitchen lights, which illumined only the stovetop and her face. She got out a skillet and some bacon and eggs, and I told her how Dave had strung me along with the sabbatical issue. As she listened, her egg-cracking became violent. I described the casual way Dave had lied about his trip to Chicago, and Audrey took out her frustration on the eggs, scrambling them far longer and with more zest than needed.

"I knew there was something weird about that call from Fresno," she muttered through clenched teeth.

I summarized Dave's story about meeting Kim in high school and how their renewed acquaintance had evolved. Audrey pushed the eggs onto two plates with dizzying speed and smacked the wooden spoon onto the counter.

As she turned to hand me my plate, I saw the dimly lit tears on her cheeks. Audrey only cries when she's enraged.

"How could that man do such horrible things? He doesn't even seem to realize it's wrong to lie and cheat! Doesn't he have a conscience? I mean, what are we supposed to tell Rachel after she's shown such commitment to keep herself pure? And because of that man's sermon!"

I looked down and took a bite.

Audrey sat across from me and wiped her cheeks with the back of her hands. "What did you say to him?"

"I got pretty frustrated. Called him a hypocrite."

Audrey reached for a napkin and blew her nose. "That's a good start."

"I didn't dare go further. He hit the wall."

Audrey leaned over and squinted at my face. The few beams from the light over the stove didn't quite reach the table. "Hit the wall?"

"Yeah. Scraped his knuckles."

She continued studying my face.

I looked up. "What? Audrey, he hit the *wall*, not me. We didn't come to blows. At least . . ."

She leaned even closer to keep eye contact while I ate my eggs. "At least what?"

"Nothing. We didn't come to blows."

"You mean he tried to hit you and missed?"

"No."

"Well, what then? What do you mean 'at least'?"

"I don't know why I said it. The whole confrontation was intense."

"You're not answering my question. Something else happened."

"Well, obviously, a lot happened."

"Something else to do with him hitting you."

I sighed and took another couple of bites. "I've never thought of myself as angry until today."

Audrey stared. "I don't understand."

"I'm an angry man."

"Well, I can see why. After what Dave's done, I'm one angry woman."

"No, no. I mean"—I finished chewing the bite that was in my mouth—"I was ready to beat him to a pulp."

Her jaw dropped. "The pastor?"

"Had my fists all set."

"So you were trying to keep from throwing punches yourself." Audrey's gaze was intense. "But you didn't. You didn't beat up the pastor."

"Not with my fists."

She looked away and shook her head. "Drop the code, Jim. I can't follow it. What are you saying?"

"I threatened him."

"You *threatened* to beat him up?"

"No." I set my fork on the plate. "He wouldn't confess the adultery, so I had to make him. I threatened to tell the board everything I knew unless he stopped lying. 'You'll have to take your chances,' I said. I made a power play and it worked, and it felt great. It was better than punching him."

Audrey's eyes went still. She retreated from her face in a way I hadn't seen for years. "Just so no one hit anybody."

"This was better."

"How can you say that?" she whispered. "I've never heard you talk this way."

"I told you. I've never thought of myself as an angry man until right now."

"You don't mean you actually took pleasure in humiliating him."

"Yes, that's exactly what I mean."

She stared at me for some time, then lowered her eyes to her plate.

I couldn't look at her. "I'm not saying I'm proud of what I did. I'm not saying I'm proud of the pleasure. I hate what I did, because it's exactly what my dad used to do. All I'm saying is that now I understand why Dad humiliated people. It's a rush. And the thing that sickens me the most is that I probably can't stop."

"You're tired. You shouldn't talk about this right now."

"I am tired, but I've never seen this more clearly. I was going to be gracious to Dave, redeem a little bit of the church's history. I was going to be bigger than all the other leaders, because I wasn't going to throw this pastor away. But Dave tricked me. He made a chump out of me. I've never been such a fool. And I can't get over it. That's what I see so clearly: I'm a small man, and even smaller for thinking I was so big."

"I don't think you're a small man. You're a good man trying to stop a nightmare."

I sneered. "I'll probably never look so good on the surface, but I've never felt so foul."

I looked at Audrey's eyes, searching for her response. But she wasn't there, and I had to look away. I finished the last of the eggs.

"So you forced him to confess through . . ."

I sat back. "Go ahead and say it. I blackmailed him."

"And then he confessed and hit the wall and you wanted to punch him." Audrey massaged her temples. "Was there an inspiring end to the evening, or was it all downhill from there?"

"Well, I wanted to know why he took up with Kim. That's when he told me the story."

"What was his excuse?"

"Didn't need one."

"Dave didn't need an excuse?" Audrey pursed her lips. "Here we go again."

"I'm just telling you—"

"More code."

"It's not code, honey. In Dave's mind, he didn't need an excuse for what he did. He had it all worked out long before he started with Kim."

Audrey snatched my plate from the table and stacked it on hers. "Suppose you just pick where the beginning is and start there."

"I don't know . . ." I dropped from sub-bellow to super whisper. "I don't know where the beginning is. You're interrogating me as if I'm Sherlock Holmes and have it all worked out. If you think this story doesn't make any sense, you haven't even heard the worst yet. The worst part is how he ministered to us for seven years, how he set us up before his adultery ever happened." I realized my fist was pressed into the table and I was practically in her face.

Her beautiful lines were contorted and she retreated even further from her eyes.

I withdrew. "You have to understand, honey, I've not only learned that my pastor's an adulterer—I've learned what he's really been teaching us. We hired a man who's probably not a Christian. And we've listened to his teaching without noticing."

Audrey didn't move. "Sorry."

"For what?"

"I'm not saying the right things this morning."

"Whatever. It's fine."

"I didn't mean to interrogate you."

"Whatever."

She looked outside at the light that seemed to have arrived suddenly. "I just thought you needed to talk. Maybe this isn't the time."

"No, no. I need to talk. It's the only chance I have to make sense of this mess. I don't know what to do."

Audrey was still looking out the window, but her hand searched for mine. She gave a quick squeeze and withdrew perceptibly even while she held on. "What's Dave been teaching that isn't Christian?"

"I don't know where to start."

"Just start anywhere. I was rude before."

"I'm not a professor, and I've never cared about this stuff until now. How am I supposed to explain it?"

"Please. If you need to talk, let's talk."

I never knew what I was waiting for at moments like this. I sighed. "All I know is, his teaching sounded like the gospel but wasn't."

"When he talked about sin and God's will and forgiveness, he didn't mean it?"

"No, that's not it." I took in the strengthening sun. "But the way you put it shows something I'm trying to understand. The fact is, Dave never talked about sin. He never talked about God's will or forgiveness, either. But when he talked, those were the words we heard."

"What did he talk about?"

"Disease, God's best, healing."

"Aren't those the same things—spiritually?"

"Close enough for us not to question what he meant. We assumed he was saying our old truths in new words. When he said 'disease' we heard 'sin.' When he said 'healing' we heard 'forgiveness.' Those are the things we talk about in church. What the younger people heard, I don't know."

"What did Dave mean by 'disease,' then?" Audrey let go of my hand and got up to make some coffee.

"He meant an illness that people catch from each other. Life leaves us wounded, unloved, needy. Our woundedness makes us do destructive things."

"Like have affairs."

"Exactly."

Audrey paused for a moment in the middle of filling the coffee filter. "Isn't that an excuse? His parents' divorce wounded him, so he gets a free pass on having an affair? I don't buy it. He still has responsibilities."

"It's not an excuse, because he agrees with you. He knows he has responsibilities, but he doesn't see the same ones as you do. His responsibility is to admit his 'needs.' Any disease can be cured, as long as you admit you've got it."

"That's it? Just admit you're needy?"

"Well, look at it from his point of view. Until their divorce, his parents looked great. They went to church, volunteered, sang solos. But Dave knew different. Whatever destroyed their marriage, Dave witnessed it daily and saw the self-deception in their church attendance."

Audrey came back to the table and sat down. "If they had just admitted there was a problem, something could've been done."

I nodded. "That's what he means by healing. There's no confession, because that would mean you intentionally did something wrong. Forgiveness is irrelevant, because all the wrongs cancel themselves out. You can't forgive something that isn't anybody's fault. So the only issue for Dave is healing. You admit there's a problem, and then you're being sincere."

"But that can't be all God requires," Audrey said. "He still has standards." She folded her arms and looked back at me. "What about Dave's own sermon about keeping sex for marriage? Doesn't he even feel defensive about it?"

"We misunderstood that sermon."

"What could we have misunderstood? Keep sex for marriage."

"He said that was 'God's best.' He didn't say it was a rule. Many of the kids had already messed up, and most of them probably will. He was saying, 'Get as close to God's best as you can.'"

"I don't think we heard the same sermon."

"I'm telling you what he told me. At the time, I heard the same sermon you heard."

"I know what he said. I don't care how he revises it now."

"He's not revising. Think back, Audrey. He went into great detail about how premarital sex harms your self-image. He talked a lot about STDs. But he never said anything like 'Fornication is wrong.' His only point was, 'It's bad for you.' We really did misunderstand him."

Audrey turned her head and looked out the window. "There's no point arguing about it now."

"I'm not arguing with you."

"Yes you are. Do you want to be Sherlock Holmes or not?"

"I'm trying to understand this, Audrey. How am I supposed to help the church if I don't understand what went wrong?"

She whispered low, whacking the air with stiff hands. "I don't see why we should even listen to him. He's a liar. He's going to destroy his wife and children. I can't be dispassionate about that."

I found myself taking her hands and turning her toward me. I couldn't look at her, but I held her hands. "I'm not dispassionate about it. I'm just numb. I can't seem to feel anything..."

I gazed at her face, searching for her. But she was gone again. What remained was a beautifully carved shape. Her cheekbones curved under her eyes. Her lips were suspended beneath her lean nose. All the smile lines were present, but hard. She was gone, and who knew how many years she would take to return.

I looked at her hands and let go.

Rachel appeared. "What are you guys doing? It's early." She stared at us.

Audrey pursed her lips at me.

I turned my head toward Rachel. "We're talking about some heavy stuff, honey."

Rachel looked at Audrey and then back at me. "Heavy?"

"Yeah, some stuff at church that I have to deal with. It's not your problem."

Audrey's mouth opened but she closed it quickly.

Rachel still stared. "Okay." She hugged herself the way girls do. "I was going to meet with Pastor Dave today."

Nausea.

"About the courtship seminar."

Mouth open, but no words.

"Remember?"

"You'd better tell her, Jim."

Rachel still stared. "Tell me what?"

This would be good practice. Tell the trustees what? Tell the congregation what? Your pastor is a liar and an adulterer? And let it sink in? "I told Pastor Dave not to come in today. He's not going to be our pastor anymore, honey."

Rachel looked at Audrey again.

My voice dropped to a whisper. "He's been in a wrong relationship."

Her eyes were all pain. "You're saying he's cheating on Amy?"

"I'm sorry, honey."

"That's impossible."

Audrey started to cry. She stood up and hugged Rachel.

Rachel pulled away and locked eyes with me. "It's impossible."

"Honey, I saw him with the other woman."

"So you're just going to throw him away?"

I looked at the floor. "Honey, we're way beyond that now. They've taken trips together—"

"With what? Pastor Dave can barely take his family on trips. It's impossible."

I froze. I stared at Rachel. "What did you say?"

Audrey hugged her again. "She's in shock, Jim."

I looked into the middle distance. "He never turned in the—"

"Sweetheart, what's the matter?"

"Daddy, where are you going? Daddy!"

18

I was at First Savings, the church's bank, when it opened. I stood at the door and watched Tim, the manager, unlock it with his left hand, his right hand holding one of the sci-fi books he read at every lull.

The church had been a customer here for decades before I became manager of the cross-town rival. When I became church treasurer years ago, it was a standing joke between Tim and me to ask about business. He would eye me with his sarcastic gaze and open with a deadpan, "How are things holding up there at the Mutual?" "Just barely." Then one of several alternate comebacks: "Always glad to hear you're surviving," or, "You can always take the church's accounts over there if you need some new customers. No hard feelings. Anything to help." We both knew my branch of the Mutual had twice the business of First Savings.

I had always liked Tim, but this morning, I wasn't in the mood for any banter. "Tim, I need a printout of every single account the church has."

He looked me up and down with a squint. "Serious?"

"Very."

He raised his eyebrows. "Let's pull them up."

He led me with his athletic gait back to the conference room and shut the door. It smelled like dead air fresheners. We sat silently as a printer whirred and pushed out paper. We had both been through this kind of thing before, and it made us angry. The banker is tricked by the criminal along with everyone else. But unlike everyone else, he gets paid not to be tricked. Even though Tim had been divorced three times, went on a bender once a month, and was always shacking up with twenty-three-year-old women—don't ask me how he got them—he maintained the highest ethical standards in the business. He flexed his hand in a nervous tic, rippling his muscles under his button-down shirt.

Account by account, line by line, page by page, I went through the financial activity of the church. Nothing. There were no unusual items. Deposits had all been regular and timely. I checked them even though I expected no irregularities on the money-collection side. The ushers and the counters were never alone with cash and checks. The activity in the checking account also looked normal. I recognized most of it. The vendors were all our usual ones. The extraordinary drafts were connected to unusual events that I recalled distinctly— plumbers, the copier repairman, the computer guru.

Tim looked up from a report he was skimming. "Anything?"

"No. Not yet." And then my eye crossed an account number I didn't recognize. A checking account. "Wait a minute. What's this?"

Tim peered across the table. "The checking account? That's the new one."

Fallen • 181

"New one?"

Tim squinted at me again. "Your pastor opened that account last spring—around the time you guys bought that acreage." I must've gone white, because Tim laughed nervously and said, "Boy, you weren't kidding when you said it was serious. I thought maybe you just suspected Eddy of raiding the poor box for his doughnut money."

I slumped in my seat.

Tim looked away. "That was a stupid crack. Sorry."

"No, no. I would've laughed." We sat in silence for a moment. Then I got in gear again. "What's this other account here, the savings account? It looks like it was opened on the same day."

Tim rolled his chair over and got out his pen to start writing things down. "Yes, the savings account. Your pastor came in shortly after the land purchase—or maybe it was the day you opened escrow." Tim looked over the activity from that period. "Yes, it was the same day. I remember now, because that transaction was a lot more complicated than it needed to be."

"More complicated?"

"Yeah." He pointed to a printout. "Here's the check the church wrote to Hank Wagner for the land: $900,000. But Dave set up the gift as an actual exchange of cash, which of course he didn't need to do. So as you see, Hank wrote a check back to the church for $100,000."

"Gift? What are you talking about? What check?"

Tim sighed and shook his head. "Okay, so your pastor is streetwise enough to play naïve." He sighed again and then went into explanatory mode. "Here's what he did, at least according to what he told me. He advised Hank that there were tax advantages to giving the church a break on the purchase price as a donation. Hank obviously liked the idea. So the church cut a check for $900,000 to Hank. Hank in turn wrote one for $100,000 to the church, cutting the amount the church really had to pay to $800,000. Your pastor came here with that check after opening escrow and said the church wanted to open a separate checking account. Said it was for a special program or something. He was a signer on the accounts and he had the incorporation papers for the church. He also brought back several signatures the next day. So we didn't question anything. But we did tell him it would be silly to keep such a large amount of money in checking. We told him he should put the majority of it in a savings account or a CD. He chose to open the savings account."

"Let me see the signature cards."

Tim went out, pulled all the church's signature cards, and returned. On the card for the new checking account were four signatures: Dave's, mine, Eddy's, and Tom's.

"That's not my signature. It's close, but it's wrong. Look at the J on the one I signed for our CD two years ago."

Tim compared the two cards. "More counts in the indictment."

I sat looking at the records, straining to internalize the enormity of what had happened.

Tim sat back in his chair. "It would be elegant if it weren't so sinister. Many crimes would be."

"*Elegant* is a good word for it. The bank couldn't have detected a problem, because Dave had all the necessary credentials and there was nothing irregular about the check he got from Hank Wagner. The new accounts would never show up on our books, because the bookkeeper would never be informed. So the $100,000 would never be missed. We were told the purchase price was $900,000, and $900,000 was what left our account. Hank would never know anything was amiss, because he would get a document from Dave, on church letter-head, acknowledging his donation for tax purposes. No one else at the church would have to know about that document. And the clincher was that none of the trustees ever met Hank. The whole matter was handled by Dave. So Hank would never have mentioned the gift to any other church officer."

"There's one other way the accounts could've been detected, though."

"What's that? The monthly statements?"

"Right."

"Dave thought of that too. A couple weeks ago, Lynn, the church secretary, was telling me how very considerate our pastor was. 'He always brings in the mail and sorts it for me,' she said."

"Very thorough."

"No kidding. So thorough, a hundred grand simply disappeared into his hands."

"And promptly started slipping through them. See, he's drawn these two accounts down to about $60,000."

"Down to sixty? Since April?"

"Yep."

I could only shake my head.

"Why was he doing it, Jim? Debts? Too much fellowship at the casino, maybe?"

"A woman. That's how I got onto this in the first place. I found out about her last night. But I only made the connection this morning. You can't take your mistress on trips to Chicago without money."

"Chicago? You'd need lots of money."

"Yeah, but forty grand in just a matter of months!"

"Hey, women are expensive. Normally, a guy's got to be careful. But not the pastor."

I sank into a numb stupor while Tim photocopied the signature cards and got waylaid by one of his tellers. I mulled over my history with Dave yet again. Had he planned this kind of embezzlement when he first asked the trustees to make him a signer? Maybe he just wanted the convenience, like he professed at the time, and the idea to embezzle occurred to him later. But it was equally possible he had deliberately laid groundwork for this scheme all those years ago. One thing was certain: It was all too clear why he had inserted himself into the negotiation with Hank—why he had mentioned Hank's land at all. It was about more than his father's old friendship. It had come within weeks of his first meeting with Kim in February. It was the first step in a detailed plan to divert church funds for his own use.

And what a use! He was going to finance his affair—finance it as long as he could. He was going to pump up his lifestyle with Kim, make the perks of his new relationship as indulgent as the relationship itself.

And what a sum! Forty grand! Here we were, six months after the deal had closed, and he had spent at a rate topping six thousand dollars a month. His heist had immediately financed the trip to Chicago. No wonder his request for more vacation time was so urgent, and his leaving so sudden. Who knew how they flew, where they stayed, what they ate, what kind of car they rented? Who knew how extensively they plundered the Magnificent Mile on a shopping spree? To a guy making forty grand a year, having a slush fund worth two and half times that must've seemed like limitless wealth.

Was she in on this? Did Kim know where the money came from to finance their luxurious living? Maybe he told her and she didn't care. That would be some kind of cold woman.

Maybe she didn't ask. Maybe she just went along to the hotels and the restaurants and just took the gifts without asking, "How can you afford this?" There again, she'd have to be pretty hardened not to ask the obvious question.

Maybe she did ask and he lied.

It didn't matter. Our pastor had taken the congregation's money.

Old people had given from their often meager retirements to fund that land purchase. I knew young families who had scraped together a hundred dollars a month for it. They'd done so faithfully for several years. One wealthy man in the church had delayed the construction of his own house for eighteen months to give more than a hundred grand. All these people had given their hard-earned dollars to ensure a future for the church.

Actually, they had given to God. They loved him and gave cheerfully what they had. It was God's own. That land fund was the only material thing I could think of that actually warranted the label "holy."

My pastor had stolen an expression of the people's love. They had not given that money so he could meet his pathetic needs and cheat on his wife. What really galled me was that he had done it for the sake of a measly hundred grand. He had hardened his heart, robbed young and old, rich and poor, destroyed his ministry, and blasphemed God, all for that paltry sum of money. At the rate of six thousand dollars a month, the amount he stole would have lasted him about eighteen months. And that was being generous. Once he got used to his new perks, his spending would've accelerated. In bringing all that guilt on himself, Dave had gained only short-lived luxuries.

It was perverse. And what had profited him so little would demolish the church.

This was the worst catastrophe in the church's history, and it had happened on my watch. It was my fault. I was so determined not to be like Dad, so determined not to use my professional standards like a club with which to beat the trustees, that I had let them make Dave a signer on all our accounts. I had let them put Dave in charge of the land deal with Hank for the same reason. I would've had to have been stubborn, and maybe even belligerent, to stop them from doing it. Just like Dad.

I had based my conduct as a church leader on the principle of "Do not unto others what Dad did." And now we were out forty grand.

The catastrophe couldn't have hit at a worse time. We had purchased the land, and now we needed to build. We needed to raise funds for a whole new physical plant. Dave's adultery by itself would've divided the congregation, pitting those who would forgive against those who would punish. Now the embezzlement would divide the people further, stoking resentment among those who had sacrificed for the fund, provoking suspicion among those who had stood on the sidelines, and launching a hunt for someone to blame among whomever was left.

The project would stall and people would leave.

And I was chairman. I would have to lead. What would they think of me when they heard about my failures? How would I lead them once they knew I'd let the trustees make Dave a signer on the church's accounts? What could I possibly do to restore their confidence?

I thought back to the sense of power I had felt the previous evening, remembering the pleasure I'd taken in knowing all these atomic secrets. I had thought I would dole out the secrets selectively—little grants of power to others. I had thought I would solve the mysteries of Dave's soul, as if I were uniquely suited for this spiritual police work. I had thought I would set precedents.

But I had known nothing. I hadn't even known of the adultery, much less the heresies Dave had concocted in his mind to justify it. And I'd had no idea of his methodical stealing.

Tim returned and slipped all the printouts and signature card copies into a manila envelope. "Do you ever wonder if your religion is real?"

It was not the sort of thing Tim had ever asked. "What do you mean?"

He pulled the tight, creased skin of his face even tighter. "Well, here's your pastor hooking up with some woman who isn't his wife. His job is to tell everybody how to be holy, but he's no better than I am. In fact, in one respect at least, I'm better. I couldn't tell you the first thing about the Bible, and I couldn't pray to save my life, but I can tell you why it's wrong to steal other people's money. And I can keep myself from doing it, even though I've got access to a lot more than a hundred grand. So if religion doesn't make even your pastor a better man, how do you know it's real?"

I spoke slowly, choosing my words with care. "You're right, Tim. A pastor should be different. Dave hasn't even kept the Ten Commandments, much less behaved like a spiritual leader. So we're going to fire him and find another pastor."

"Yeah, but how do you know your religion is real? What if the other pastors are just better fakes?"

"I've known a lot of pastors, and I've never seen one like Dave."

"You thought he was pretty good until yesterday. The others could've been even smoother."

"Yeah, but they can't all have had secret lives."

Tim shrugged his square shoulders as he stood over me. "Why not? Everybody has a secret life. Maybe a chat room friend, maybe just a fantasy. Pastors are no different. So if their heads don't work any better than anyone else's, how can you say that your religion accomplishes anything?"

"I can't *prove* Christianity to your satisfaction."

Tim waved his hand. "I don't care about proof. I'm talking about reality."

"That's just it. I can show you a bunch of people who changed when Christ came into their lives. But you'll always be able to find someone to prove that Christ doesn't make any difference."

He lasered me with his eyes. "I don't care about proof."

"Well, you asked why Christianity is real—"

"Uh-uh. I asked how you *know.*"

"Me?" I stared at a pencil holder. "I guess I've never questioned whether it was real."

"So you don't know."

"Come on, Tim. Do you seriously believe you only know what you've questioned?"

"Yeah. I do believe that." He held up the envelope. "This tells you why. When people don't ask questions, they get screwed." He sat down and looked out the window. "But there's got to be more to your religion than habit. What's going to take you back to church now that your pastor's going to jail?"

"My own experience. I know Christ is real. What somebody else does, what Dave does, changes nothing."

Tim trained his X-ray vision on a pedestrian crossing the street. Then he nodded. "I'll buy that."

I sighed. "But this whole mess is as much my fault as Dave's."

Tim's eyes came back to mine. "What are you talking about?"

"Dave was preaching garbage for seven years and I didn't pay any attention. Maybe that wouldn't matter to you. But there were administrative things I allowed to happen that would concern you. I knew it was wrong to make Dave a signer on the accounts. I knew we shouldn't delegate the land negotiation to him. I let those things slide."

"Doesn't make it your fault. The pastor's the thief."

"Yeah, but in discovering Dave's sins, I've discovered my own. I thought I was smart. I thought I could make the church run better than leaders in the past. That's the sin of pride."

Tim's face creased in a way that almost smiled. "Who made me your priest?"

"There's more, padre. Anger, brawling."

"Brawling?"

"Well, close to it. I was ready to beat him up last night—for what he's doing to his kids."

Tim leaned forward and smiled for real. "You almost beat up your pastor?"

I looked down at the tattered cuffs on my windbreaker. "Yeah. As it was, I practically had to blackmail him to tell the truth."

Tim still smiled. "That must've been fun. Always wanted to do that."

"It was fun. I hate myself for how much I enjoyed it."

"My son, go have a few drinks."

"No, seriously. This is the worst time in my church's history, and the only resources I have are pride and anger. How can I know Christ is in my life when I'm so full of sin? That's not a problem you're going to care about. But it's what I'm dealing with today."

"Drinks won't help, I guess."

"Nope."

"So what are you going to do? Leave the church?"

"This isn't about the church. It's about me. I can't leave myself. I wonder what a guy like Moses did when he failed. How did he—?" I looked at my confessor. "Tim, I think you may have shown me my whole problem. Moses—"

I didn't get a chance to explain. Tim's face tightened and he stood up. I looked where he was staring and saw Dave walking from his car to the bank.

I bounded out of the conference room and stood facing the glass front doors. Dave approached, looked through the glass, and we locked eyes. His surprise turned to hesitation. I held up the envelope Tim had given me and glared at Dave in fury. He stared at the envelope. His hesitation turned to comprehension, and then to fear. He bolted to his car.

With a phone to my ear, calling the police, I watched him peel out of the parking lot.

19

From the bank, I drove directly to Dave's house. His car wasn't there. The home that usually looked so full of life—as if all the toys and cups and food had been dropped in the wake of some fresh excitement—now had the appearance of desertion, as if everything had been dropped because there was no more reason to play.

I went to the front door and rang the bell.

When Amy answered, she was pale, and there was no activity in her eyes—not grief, not shock, not even anger. Her cheeks were slack and her lips flat. Where before there had been so much nimble irony, now there was nothing. Her face had died.

She took a step back into the entry hall, but said nothing.

I looked at my feet. "You know where Dave is?"

She shook her head. "He left us."

"When?"

"Early this morning."

"Did he say anything?"

"More than I could handle in fifteen minutes."

"Fifteen minutes? He told you everything in fifteen minutes?"

She nodded and looked down the street. "When I opened my eyes this morning, he was folding a T-shirt. He just looked at me for a while, and then he zipped up the bag. He said he had to get out of here. He said our marriage was dead and he'd found someone else. He needed to figure out what to do. He was quitting the church. He kissed the kids . . ."

I waited, but she was finished. "I don't know what to say. I'm sorry."

She looked back at me. "Do you know where he is?"

"No. I'm looking for him." Best to leave the matter there. "Can we do anything? Take the kids somewhere?"

"No."

I fidgeted with the zipper on my jacket. "We're with you, Amy. The church is with you, whatever happens. We're on your side."

She compressed her lips in acknowledgment. "It's too soon, Jim. I don't know what my side is."

I nodded.

In the gloom of the living room, I now saw Amanda, perched on the edge of the couch, swinging her legs.

I nodded again to Amy, mumbled something about how I would let her know what I found, and walked back out to the driveway.

I sat for unrecorded minutes in my car, desolated. I knew this was only one encounter of many. And the ones to come would be far longer and more intense. I would meet with the trustees that night. I would inform them and absorb their reactions, and we would agonize over what to do. Then we would face the congregation and repeat the story. We'd fumble for some way to answer the shock and grief, knowing that there is no way to respond rationally to adultery, theft, abandonment, and deceit.

I shuffled into work aware of Flynn's eyes following me to my office. I grabbed a cup of coffee and turned to find her leaning against the doorframe, eyebrow arched.

I took a sip. "What's the matter?"

"Something about the stubble and the bed head just doesn't do it for me."

"Oh." I ran my fingers through what was left of my hair.

"But the sweatpants are a nice touch."

"I decided I like casual Friday."

"It's Thursday."

I tried to keep a light tone. "I'm the boss. I can declare casual Friday on Thursday if I want."

Her eyebrow sagged. "So who writes you up for being late?"

"I'll write myself up."

She smiled with her mouth, but her eyes probed. After some uncomfortable seconds of silence, she shut the door and sat down. She seemed to look me over and her voice was tentative. "Jim, you look awful."

"You said that already."

"No, I mean . . ." She tossed her hair behind her shoulder. "You seem like something's really wrong."

I turned away from the door so that no one outside would see my face through the glass. "Something is really wrong." I rubbed my eyes and glanced at Flynn, her face now craned toward mine. "You know my pastor."

"Dave?"

"I discovered yesterday he's having an affair with some realtor."

"Dave's having an affair?" She crinkled her nose. "Black hair, kind of bouncy?"

I started. "That's her. How'd you know?"

She shook her head and looked outside. "They've been pretty thick at the Bean."

I held my face in my hands.

"I'm sorry."

I lifted my face again. She had pulled back, her eyes cautious. I told her the short version of the previous night and she edged closer again.

"Jim, that's just terrible."

"Just came from seeing his wife."

Flynn compressed her lips. "She knows?"

"She knows he's been cheating on her. But there's more." I kept my back to the door, throwing sidelong glances at Flynn. "Dave stole forty grand from the church. Had access to sixty more."

She remained still, only her eyes widening and her lips parting.

"Found out this morning." I distilled his scheme into a few sentences.

"Oh, Jim. You must be devastated."

I felt my lower lip stiffen and looked away.

"You were so close to Dave."

I still couldn't talk.

She slowly reached across the desk and rested her hand on my forearm.

"I was trying to help him but he tricked me."

She took my hand and leaned in to see my face. Her scent came into my consciousness.

"I gave him chances, even when I knew he was lying. He kept tricking me. What do you do with someone who won't take another chance?"

She squeezed my hand and held on.

There was a sudden warmth inside my neck and shoulders that I hadn't felt in years. I'd forgotten. "This was my chance to get it right, to make the church a gracious place. It'll never happen now."

Flynn shook her head and her hair swung off her shoulder and graced my wrist. "You don't know that."

"I do know it. You have no idea how vicious church people are."

"I know nuns."

"They've got nothing on Baptists."

She sighed a laugh. "Okay, maybe not. But you're still forgetting something."

"What?"

"You only know what they'll do without you."

"What do you mean, without me?"

She smiled and stared me down over the rim of her glasses. "Without the master, of course they'll be petty. But you don't know how they'll respond to a good dose of Jim. A few of them may learn the secrets."

I stared. "What secrets?"

"How to treat people. How to help them do their best. No one taught me the secrets in college. You did, just by expecting more of me than I expected of myself. And by putting up with me."

I kept staring at her unlined face, for once purged of sarcasm.

Her eyes dropped. "I guess I haven't told you how much . . . um, how much you mean to all of us." Her eyes came back to mine. "If you're in charge, I know the people at your church will learn, too."

I could feel my lower back relaxing against my chair. "I wish I could believe that."

"That's what you do. You get the best out of people."

"Not lately."

"Well, maybe not with Dave. I know you tried to turn him around. But what he did is not your fault." Her grip on my hand persisted.

I sighed and took a tentative glance over my shoulder at the door. "I've never been humiliated like this, Erin."

"How have you been humiliated? You tried to help a guy and he didn't respond."

"I was tricked. I'm supposed to be smarter than that. Plus, everything I believed has been destroyed, and I have nothing to replace it with."

"This isn't the time to reevaluate your whole life."

"Maybe not."

"You need to get some rest. You need to go home."

I glared at her. Why was she sending me home? If I'd wanted to go home, I wouldn't have come to the office. There was no comfort at home, no one to listen. How was I going to explain the embezzlement to Audrey?

Flynn retreated under my glare. But she didn't release my hand. "Or maybe going home wouldn't be restful."

I stared out the window, down the street toward the Bean, feeling a new nausea. "You're probably right. I need to go home." I looked back at her. "Thanks for listening."

"No problem." She squeezed my hand again, released it, and stood to leave. "And Jim? I meant what I said."

I walked out of the branch, knowing that all eyes were on me. Tammy turned abruptly back to the drive-up window. Crystal looked at me, then at Flynn. Melissa smiled at me as I passed, but her eyes reverted to Flynn too. In my mind's eye, Mom tracked me with her grieving stare. They had seen. They had all seen.

20

The wilderness expanded before me and I was being pursued. The scrutiny of all the girls in the office was not intense enough to affect me this way. If Rachel had seen, her gaze would singe me, but not like this. Even if Audrey had seen, I would not be shaken the way I was now. No, I was being pursued by one who knew the depths of my infidelity. The crackle of his presence was almost audible. It seemed I could feel the heat of his breath on the back of my neck, rising up to my face.

I'd seen a young wife with death on her face. I'd seen an abandoned child, sitting aimlessly swinging her feet. I'd been deceived by the adulterer myself and angered by his deception. And yet my assistant merely touches my hand and I turn my heart over to her.

I'd seen Dave's hatred of Amy, and I had lectured him. Yet a little sympathy from my subordinate overwhelms years of my wife's devotion—and I'm angry at Audrey for knowing me so intimately.

Day after day I'd worked diligently to avoid even the appearance of impropriety, only now to find sin rooted in the very depths of my soul.

He knew. He saw. I could see his pillar of fire towering over me.

I walked out the door and approached the Camry. The glossy white paint seemed to mock the blackness in my heart. I slumped in the driver's seat with my foot slack against the ground.

Again I remembered Moses. What did he do to survive? My mind clawed for deep-rooted words. The verses I'd heard since childhood became pleas—my pleas. I decided to face the fire.

"I'm dead, Lord. You've found me here, confiding in a woman who is not my wife, feeding off of her sympathy. You know how far back, and how deep, my disloyalty goes, and you know where it leads. You saw me pursue Flynn from her very first day at the bank. The sharpness of her wit caught my attention, and she looked good to me. I nurtured a personal rapport—did it deliberately—and today I reaped what I've sown.

"Now I want her even more. Her touch is still on my hand. I revel in the sound of her voice, and the way she tosses back her hair and looks at me over the rims of her glasses with those eyes. I'm thirsty for her admiration—from someone so hard to impress, and yet so impressionable. No one else knows how I've stoked this desire, but I cannot hide it from you. I cultivated this wickedness in your presence, and it sickens me to think that I'm just like Dave. He's ahead of me on the path, and he's crossed a boundary that I haven't trespassed yet. But I can't deny that my path is the same.

"How did I become this walking lie?"

My sight came back into focus and I looked through the windshield into the bank a few feet away. Despite the dimness of the interior, I could see Melissa's eyes on me. Why was I sitting in my Camry with the door open, staring at nothing? Bad enough that I'd shown up unshaven and in sweatpants. The girls were probably speculating about my hitting the bottle. I shut the door and started the engine.

And then I saw, with searing clarity, what I had done.

I'd created a man called Professional Jim; a man who would never sit in his car like this. Professional Jim always knew where he was going next and why. I'd given him swagger and ease, endowed him with an ability to command the personalities around him. I'd created him to give myself power. When I switched him on, I didn't have to think or examine my motives. He simply did what was right. When I switched him off, I could rest from my labors and see that my work was very good.

Except at home.

I tried not to switch him off when I went home. But I usually did, absentmindedly assuming I was fine without him. Truth is, I wasn't. I got angry, bullied, bellowed. And when I switched Professional Jim back on to fix my blunders, it was too late. I needed to be Professional Jim in every situation or I couldn't be the awesome husband and father that I fancied myself.

"But, Lord, it's like the switch is broken now and I can't turn him back on."

I backed out of my parking space, and as I turned into the driving lane, there was the Bean. I navigated the obstacle course of curbs and speed bumps and parked again. The

Camry chirped as I automatically set the alarm, and I went in to get some coffee. The music seemed especially loud because hardly anybody was there, but the chaos of a rush was still obvious: chairs and newspapers scattered, a crumpled napkin on the floor near the trash can, cocoa and cinnamon powder spilled at the creamer station, cups and coffee rings on every surface.

"Hey, Jim! Day off?" True to form, Lisa was fully caffeinated and ready to serve.

"You might say that."

"Tall Italian?"

"Thanks."

"No problem!" Thumbs up, a little squeeze of the fist for emphasis. "Where's Dave? Haven't seen him today."

I fumbled with my money clip. "I was hoping you could tell me."

"Sorry! Guess that means you get his table." Lisa handed me a hot mug. Then her face popped. "Wait! Here's Kim! Maybe she knows where he is. Hey, Kim!"

"Lisa!" The sound was long and melodic, with a very cool rasp just behind the tone. I could see now she was all jazz from her feet to her hair.

"We were just wondering where Dave is. Grande mocha?"

Kim shot an inadvertent glance at Dave's table. "Yeah, grande. I thought Dave would be here."

"Nope."

Kim caught me staring. "You know Dave too?"

I let too many beats go by. "Yeah, well . . ."

She glanced at my sneakers and a look of amusement came into her eyes. "Say, don't you run the bank over there?"

"You'd never know it today."

Kim laughed. "Well, I was going to say it looks like we're taking the casual thing a little far. My name's Kim, by the way."

"Jim." I realized I was nodding as if to say, "Yup, that's m'name." We shook hands and she glanced again at Dave's table.

Lisa set down the mocha. To go.

Kim took the cup and smiled neon at me. "Great meeting you, Jim! I'm sure you clean up real nice. Bye, Lisa!" She pushed open the door with her elbow and with her free hand drew out her cell.

Lisa and I looked at each other and her face was tight. Then she laughed and shrugged her shoulders. I shuffled over to Dave's table, lowered myself into his chair, pulled up a section of newspaper, and hunched over it, but my mind ran back to God.

"Lord, Professional Jim won't switch back on because he failed where he was supposed to be strongest—at church. With Dave, my gimmicks were worse than useless. Every trick I used put me more at his mercy. Tell him to be smarter! Give him hope! Hold him accountable! Professional Jim is a broken man, a shell."

I looked up from the paper and stared across the parking lot toward the bank.

But this morning, Flynn had given him back to me: "They just need a dose of Jim," she'd said. "They'll learn the secrets from the master." Her words were hallucinogenic to me, and all the more powerful because she believed them.

"Maybe she has feelings for Professional Jim. Maybe that's what she almost said: 'I guess I haven't told you how much . . . I love you.' I know that's what she meant. She was unbuttoning her feelings. If we hadn't been at the office, she would have told me.

"And why shouldn't she feel that way? I've had an impact on her. She really has learned from me. I mean, her decision-making is a hundred times better than when she started. It used to be she could analyze problems—they taught her that in college—but she couldn't solve them. And she couldn't get people on board to make the solutions real. But she can do it now, because I showed her. Why shouldn't she . . ."

I watched the taillights of Kim's Mercedes as she turned the corner.

"I got Professional Jim back, all right. Flynn resurrected him in my sick soul. It doesn't matter whether she loves this pathetic fraud, because I certainly do."

I looked back at the bank in time to see Tammy emerge for her break. There she stood, smoking and staring fixedly at the Camry, resting from its fifty-yard drive.

In that instant, Professional Jim died again—exposed for who he really was. The real Jim wasn't upright, self-sufficient, and loving. The real Jim was a pitiable man who was afraid to go home, who needed his assistant to prop him up and make his fantasies real. The real Jim had an adulterous and lying heart behind his carefully cleaned up and respectable façade. I glanced down at my sweatpants and shook my head. "Perfect."

When my gaze returned to Tammy, she was looking back inside the bank at someone and tilting her head toward the Camry.

"Lord, I'm nothing but a temporary man—whatever is needed at the moment. That's how I became such a lie. If it suits me to dream about Audrey's face, then my yearning is real enough. But if it suits me to flatter the girls at the bank, to flirt, to coax their admiration, then my charm is just as authentic. I draw satisfaction from Rachel's achievements and her missteps both. I was ready to give Dave chances or to blackmail him, whichever was more to my advantage.

"But Temporary Man couldn't handle it when the problems multiplied, and now I can't find my core. The fidelity and competence I project is light on a screen, not skin and muscle.

"I even used grace as a weapon. It put people in my debt. I gave Melissa grace because she would work, not because she would profit. And Flynn, all that I invested in her—do I dare say the words?—maybe I thought that benevolent power is the best aphrodisiac.

"And now all my devices have borne fruit. Her teasing is mine, her satisfying surrenders when I remind her who she was 'pre-Jim,' her payment of adoration. All mine.

"Or is she just trying to make me feel better, the way a girl does? Maybe she sees me as a poor old man, good at heart but beaten down, and she unveils her sweet side to cheer me up. Maybe she's not showing adoration at all. Maybe it's pity.

"It can't be! I know her. She's too ironic for sympathy. There would be an edge there, and I'd see it. Besides, she knows me. She wouldn't just pat my shoulder to make me feel better. She knows I'd never buy it from her. What she and I have . . ."

Tammy went back inside.

"What she and I have . . . is *nothing*, Lord. It's dust. I am the grass of the field, sucking whatever moisture is in the clay of my soul. 'In the morning it flourisheth, and groweth up; in the evening it is cut down, and withereth.'

"'Thou turnest man to destruction; and sayest, Return, ye children of men.' I'm no different from Adam and the lying patriarchs, the angry Moses, and the wandering Israelites.

The lusting David. I'm no different from Dad, no different from the bitter leaders of the past. They were all cursed, and now I'm just like them, at the mercy of my sin's consequences.

"My plans are so heinous, I won't even admit them to myself, much less open them to the sun. But 'thou hast set our iniquities before thee, our secret sins in the light of thy countenance.' All my days are now 'passed away in thy wrath.' I've spent my years 'as a tale that is told,' and I am 'consumed by thine anger.'"

My body was pumping with adrenaline. I left my coffee and walked back outside to the Camry. *What can I do when I am cursed?* I turned the ignition and headed home.

"'Lord, thou hast been our dwelling place in all generations.' You formed this earth. You brought forth the mountains. None of the things that change this world can change you— not evil, not stupidity. Not even the cataclysms of our lives can alter you. 'From everlasting to everlasting, thou art God.'

"I've been alive for fifty years—the majority of my life is spent. My strength is all 'labor and sorrow.' Maybe I'll get my threescore years and ten—maybe fourscore. But the end is certain. I will be cut off and fly away.

"Is there any chance I can settle grace and truth in my heart in these final twenty or thirty years? I fear there isn't. I see the destruction unfolding around me, all the wrath you've troubled us with, and I know it's not the full measure of what you can do. 'Who knoweth the power of thine anger? Even according to thy fear, so is thy wrath.'

"*Wrath.* What a foreign word! I don't think I've heard that word in a sermon for years, maybe decades. All I've heard lately is that you aren't angry, you don't judge, and you don't condemn.

"But I can't understand what is happening as anything other than a taste of your wrath. The sin I nurtured in my deepest thoughts was something you allowed. I don't believe even Dave's lawlessness has been beyond your control. You've permitted him to do these things. But it can't be a sign of your blessing that our pastor has sinned and that we will now wander in the aftermath of what he's done.

"The thought is horrible—almost unspeakable. But I survey my sin alongside everyone else's, and I come to the conclusion that you've cursed us because we deserve it.

"So is there any chance for me, even now, to find grace and truth in the last years of my life? Can I ever return to my dwelling place in you? What if I could number the days left in my life; what would be the crucial things for me to ask of you? To know those things and pursue them—that would be wisdom.

"Please, Lord, let me place my requests at your feet. I ask you to come back to me. I feel I'm too far gone to return to you, Lord, so will you return to me? Track me, grip me firmly, and lead me by the hand through this desert.

"I don't deserve to be freed from this curse. Neither does anyone else. We're getting what we deserve. If you come back to us with still more wrath, we're finished.

"So I ask you to give us what we don't deserve. Mercy.

"And, please, show me how your return will affect the next generation. I want a glimpse of how your grace and truth will be established, how you will solidify it. Show me how my first fifty years can be redeemed. Show me in Rachel. Show me in the future leaders of the church."

I rushed into my empty house, grabbed Dad's Bible off the shelf in my study, and scrambled for Psalm 90. Was there any hope that my prayers would be answered? Did I have any grounds for expecting God to help me?

I stared at the page. There, in Dad's steady hand, was a date—April 17, 1967—and a neat bracket around verse 15: "Make us glad according to the days wherein thou hast afflicted us, and the years wherein we have seen evil."

21

"So our pastor's having an affair."

Mike said it and looked at Eddy, who didn't look back.

Eddy had been chairman of the church many times, but Mike never had. The two had grown up together, played high school ball together, built lives in their hometown together. Eddy had been the leader—the initiator in boyhood, the quarterback in high school, the jovial networker in adulthood. Eddy was a leader because he was likeable, and Mike was the kind of guy who followed leaders like Eddy. Loyally.

Not to say that Eddy took a visible role in public meetings, or even offered a lot of ideas. He never appeared to push anything. That was part of his skill. In the banter before a meeting, Eddy would be a major player—teasing the guys, laughing his throaty laugh, and making openings for the guys to tease him. But once a meeting officially started, Eddy would sit hunched over the table, with his mouth slightly open, writing notes. He let the other guys bulldog the issues—like Mike and the basement carpet—until he felt the time was right. When he was ready, he'd tell a story, a bit of history maybe, and usher the group toward a decision.

It always appeared effortless, and there didn't seem to be anything malicious in this tactic. Eddy was just smart.

Mike looked at me. "An affair! That's awful. We sure don't need that right now."

I was already beginning to feel dismay at the results of my just-the-facts reporting. I'd spent twenty minutes on what I'd thought was a carefully prepared account of Dave's lies. I'd spent the afternoon crafting the presentation so that his deceit would stand out—like the car ride that happened in February rather than Tuesday, and the strategic obscurity about whether his family would go to Chicago. I wanted the guys to see not only that Dave was carrying on with Kim, but that he'd lied to me—that he had lied elaborately and with calculation.

I tried to guide Mike back to the point. "Yeah, it's true. We don't need that right now. But the point is, we have a liar on our hands. Dave has been manipulating us."

"Well, sure."

Mike said it as if lying were ordinary. He may have meant that he expected an adulterer to lie. But I hadn't been surprised by the lying itself; I'd been shocked by the strategies *behind* the lying. In spite of my presentation, Mike didn't seem to see anything remarkable, except the affair.

Tom, still in his UPS uniform, stared at Mike with his eyebrows knitted. His look was almost assertive. Time to move on.

"Well, there's more to this. It gets worse, so hold your horses." They sank in their seats.

I told them about the embezzlement, summarizing how Dave had taken advantage of his position as a signer and his authority to negotiate with Hank Wagner. I couldn't help rubbing their noses in it. I told how Dave had maneuvered Hank into writing a check donating money back to the church, how Dave had then opened the two new accounts, and how he kept them secret by forging signatures and intercepting the monthly statements. Then I told them that Dave had taken $40,000 over the last six months. I concluded with Dave's dramatic arrival at the bank while Tim and I were talking, and his speedy exit.

"We really don't need that!" Mike looked at Eddy again.

I allowed the silence to lengthen. Mike shook his head repeatedly, now looking around at the other guys. Eddy was writing some notes. Jake stared at the table, while Earl maintained his eyes on the ceiling. Dick sat with his shoulders raised over his folded arms, working his jaw. Tom looked at me.

Dick finally broke the silence. "He's got to pay that back!"

Jake pulled his gaze away from the table and looked at Eddy. "And he's going to be out of the pulpit for a while, that's for sure."

"I don't know," Earl said. He had a way of delivering his favorite phrase so that it was more like a sigh than a sentence. His eyes would flit around the room without his head moving, as if he were a cornered animal. Then he'd unload another "I don't know," like a weary protest, and return his gaze to the ceiling.

I tossed my pen on the table and sat back in my chair. "Guys, what do you mean? Pay it back? Out of the pulpit for a while? Help me out, here."

Dick shifted his whole body to face me without unfolding his arms. "He's got to pay back that forty grand, of course. That's obvious. There have to be some consequences for his actions. Everybody gets off too easy these days, and it's high time we did something about it."

I stared at the notes I had made so carefully, trying to think of a diplomatic response. "Well, Dick, I agree Dave's got to face some consequences, but—"

Jake cut in. "And another one of those consequences has to be that he leaves the pulpit for a while. A good six months. Not a day less! That boy needs counseling. I've always thought so. Just couldn't ever say anything." Then Jake stopped and raised his hand, as if making a concession. "Now, I admit, he's a super-nice kid. A prince of a guy. Wouldn't deny that for a minute. Dave's just like my son—nice kid, means no harm, but wayward. He's got some kind of emotional something-or-other going on and he needs counseling. We're going to have to get a little tough with the boy this time. Just like my son."

I wasn't sure I wanted to know. "What do you mean, Jake? How did you get tough with your son? You send him to counseling?"

"Oh, tougher than that! A few years ago when he got that second divorce, I sat him down in our living room and told him straight: 'You're not coming back home this time. Your mother can't handle the stress anymore. You're forty-one, you've only been on your own ten years in your whole life, and even those years didn't all come at once. It's time you stayed out there in the cruel world. We'll set you up in an apartment and everything, pay for some school if that's what you want. But you can't come back to your room. It's tough, but that's the way it is.'"

Jake paused and wiped his nose. "Well, that was a pretty unpleasant conversation. But you know what? Things have really turned around for that boy. He studied filmmaking for a while, and even though it didn't turn into a career, I think it helped keep his mind off the ex-wives. Now he's managing the McDonald's. Good, steady work. It pays to lay down the law sometimes. That's all I'm saying."

Earl did the thing with his eyes. "I don't know."

I stared at my notes again, as if they contained useful information for where this conversation was headed. "Look, guys. Maybe I didn't make the situation clear. Dave is gone. Remember? He saw me at First Savings and split. I went over to his house and Amy told me he'd left the family. He's flown the coop."

Mike brightened. "Oh! He quit! That's probably for the best."

"No, Mike, he didn't quit. He fled. He's committed crimes here, for Pete's sake. There's a warrant out for his arrest. He's a fugitive of justice. There's no question of Dave ever coming back to the pulpit, not even after six months. Remember? I've already called the police and they're looking for him. Got his license plate number and everything. He won't pay back the forty grand, because he'll probably be in jail. See, what I'm trying to say is, you guys want to get tough on him in ways that are irrelevant now. And I don't think your ideas would've been tough enough anyway."

Mike looked at Eddy. "Not tough enough?"

"Not nearly. You don't deal with forgery and embezzlement by making the thief pay the money back. You don't deal with an adulterous pastor by putting him in counseling for a while. Those measures don't address the issues."

"I don't know."

Mike was getting real nervous, throwing more frequent glances at Eddy, who continued looking blankly at his notepad on the table.

Dick unfolded his arms and waved his hands. "Well, Dave's gone now. Not our problem. Guess we need to get a search committee together."

My heart dropped into the basement. "Uh, eventually, yeah. But, guys, I think there's a lot of other stuff to deal with first."

Now Jake was also looking at Eddy, but he addressed his question to me. "What do you mean, 'other stuff'? We've got to have a pastor. What other stuff is there?"

Tom was now slumped in his chair. Jake, Dick, and Mike were flashing glances back and forth, alternating between Eddy and one another. Earl resumed counting the little holes in the ceiling tiles.

"What other stuff is there, Jake? Well, there's Amy. How are we going to help her and the kids? What are our responsibilities? Then there's Dave himself. We'll have to press charges and go through a trial—unless he pleads guilty, of course."

"Trial?"

"Press charges?"

"I don't know."

"And last but not least, there's the congregation. We're going to have to lead them through this crisis."

Jake slapped the table. "Exactly! We'll lead them by finding another pastor. That means a search committee."

I took a deep breath and set my voice. "Not yet. The congregation is going to have a lot of questions when they hear about the adultery and the embezzlement. They'll be grieving, and probably suspicious."

Mike now looked frantically at Eddy. "Who says they're going to hear about anything?"

I studied Eddy, who continued to write steadfastly on his pad. I looked at each old man's face, searching, but they all eluded my eyes—except for Tom. He stared at me, unconscious of the curl in his lip. Something wasn't being said, but I didn't know what. How could I discover what they were hiding?

I turned my body to face Mike head-on. "*I* say they're going to hear about it—all of it. This is their pastor we're talking about, their shepherd. They are the ones who called him to this church, not us. They are the ones who entrusted the church's money to our stewardship. They are the ones we failed when we made Dave a signer on the church accounts and put him in charge of negotiating the land purchase. This is their church. We are accountable to them, and we will report to them."

Mike tried to maintain eye contact with me, but he involuntarily flicked his eyes toward Eddy.

Dick cut in. "So you're going to tell those people the pastor is having an affair and he stole forty grand."

"We are going to report it, yes, along with the decisions we made that opened the bank accounts to him."

"You're going to throw that information out there like a hand grenade and just watch it explode in your face?"

"Dick, the congregation has to hear the truth!" I was back to bellowing.

Jake huffed. "All they need to know is that their pastor quit. We're not going to tell them any more than that."

Mike jumped back in. "If we tell them everything, Dave'll sue us. I've heard of two, three churches that got sued by their pastors. He could get us for slander or something."

"From jail?" I was still facing toward Mike. "Dave's going to sue us for telling the congregation what he did? His trial's going to be in the newspaper. Let him sue!"

Dick almost growled. "We're not going to press charges. That's crazy. You may as well take out an ad saying we aren't a safe place to donate money!"

Jake nodded, and Mike muttered his approval.

Earl sighed. "I don't know."

I held up my hands and took another breath. Reset my voice. "Let me be sure I understand this. You're saying that this board shouldn't do or say anything about Dave's adultery, his abandonment of his wife and kids, or his theft of forty grand. Not a thing. We shouldn't prosecute, we shouldn't report to the people. We just say, 'Folks, our pastor quit. Let's form a search committee.'"

"You got it!" Jake smiled at the others and laughed.

"And how are we going to explain why Amy's home alone with the kids? How will we handle the next quarterly financial report? Just hope no one notices?"

Dick looked away. "Amy would probably be more comfortable in another church. She's only going to feel embarrassed sticking around here."

Jake nodded. "She needs to move on."

Tom stared at Jake and Dick, getting redder in the face with each of their remarks. Earl closed his eyes. Tight.

My jaw was slack.

At this point, Eddy looked up. He smiled gently and began to use his maple-syrup voice. "Maybe we ought to review a little history. Don't you think, fellas?" Mike, Dick, and Jake nodded. Earl almost seemed to be in pain, slowly sucking air through his teeth. "See, Jim, the five of us have been through all this before. It's been a long time, way back in '67, and almost nobody knows about it. But I think we know how to handle this current matter. Remember Pastor Schneider? You were just a boy, I think."

"The one who stomped out of a congregational meeting threatening to resign?"

"Yeah. That's him. You remember that night, huh? Well, there were reasons why it happened. About a year before that meeting, we found out he'd been involved with a lady he'd been counseling. I forget her name. You remember that lady's name, Jake?"

"Nope."

"Well, Pastor Schneider was involved with her. Just like this deal with Dave. And it came out that he'd been taking money from petty cash now and again to buy her little presents. Not as much money as Dave took, you understand, but he took it nevertheless. A few hundred dollars."

Jake pressed his finger into the table. "And that was back in the days when a hundred dollars was a hundred dollars!"

"That's right, Jake. So the board at that time had quite a lot on its plate. As far as we knew, this had never happened in the church before, so we had nothing to go by, no precedent to follow. There were some who wanted to do what you're recommending now, Jim. Tell the people everything. I was one of those at the beginning. But the older men were not in favor of that. Old Mr. Baumgartner, Dorothy's father, was chairman then. And I remember what he said like it was yesterday. He said, 'If you tell the people, they'll eat you alive.'

"That was the end of it. 'They'll eat you alive.' We didn't say any more about reporting everything to the people. Well, most of us didn't. The board just admonished Pastor Schneider that this was not God-honoring behavior and he needed to knock it off. We told him to pay back the money he'd taken and not see this lady anymore. Then we sent him away for a while with his family— three months, maybe. Called it a sabbatical or something. Pastor Schneider did everything we asked him to do—stopped carrying on with the lady, paid back the money, and everything. Took it like a man, I must say. We put it to the lady that she might be more comfortable in another setting, which she accepted very graciously.

"See, with that approach it all turned out fine. No rowdy meetings, no splits, no families heading off to other churches."

Eddy refreshed his smile. "But back to the meeting you remembered, when old Schneider stormed out. Your dad was on the board when all this happened. It was his first time. He disagreed with Old Baumgartner. Wanted to tell everybody the whole thing, even after the chairman had spoken. Got pretty hot under the collar—I think it was mainly the money part that bothered him. Anyway, your dad resigned when it didn't go his way and never did come back on the board. Ever—in spite of being invited many times by me personally. After he resigned, he told the pastor that any honorable man would've left the ministry.

"After that, your dad—and I mean no offense, Jim, because I respected your dad greatly—but he kind of bulldogged the finances. That was why Pastor Schneider walked out of that meeting a year later. He was hurt, I guess. Not that your dad was at fault. On the contrary, he never said a word about the matter to anyone. That was to his credit.

"But I tell you this because it'll give you some perspective on why this board isn't going to reveal this business of Dave's to the congregation. We need level heads right now, and I know you appreciate that."

Now Tom's jaw went slack. Earl's mouth tugged to one side.

I sat for a moment looking at the five trustees, much the way Dad must've done all those years ago. My early life suddenly made a lot more sense: Dad's anger, his inability to restrain it, wasn't pride at all. It was indignation. His rants about reporting improprieties weren't motivated by a professional contempt for amateurs. They were rants against an injustice that had never been redressed and that he feared would happen again.

My decision was now as clear as it was ever going to be, and my mind was restored to calm by that clarity. "Eddy, I thank you for the history. It does help me a great deal. I don't judge anything you guys may have done in the past. I wasn't there. But I have to disagree with your conclusion tonight. You said this board will not report Dave's offenses. You forget that I am chairman now I say we will report it."

Dick huffed. "We're in the majority, Jim."

Tom ground his teeth and Earl winced.

"Yes, you are. But as chairman of the church, I do not need your consent to call a congregational meeting. I don't need your consent to run that meeting, to have the roll called, to declare that we have a quorum, or to have the minutes read. I don't need your consent to make motions for the membership to vote on. And, as a man, I do not need your consent to tell the congregation all that I have witnessed."

Mike shot up. "They'll eat you alive! You can't do that!"

"How exactly are you going to stop me?"

Mike, Dick, and Jake all looked at Eddy. Tom and Earl froze. But Eddy just wrote on his pad.

No one breathed a word for some time. I waited a few moments longer, and then gave my verdict. "I will call a meeting of the congregation for this Sunday evening. I will report Dave's offenses and make a motion that he be terminated. I will take questions and lead the discussion. You're all welcome to stand with me. But if none of you do, I will go ahead alone. The people of this church deserve to be taken into the confidence of the leadership. They may indeed eat me alive. People may leave. The community may laugh and criticize. The new building may be delayed. But all those things can heal. Unconfessed sin never can. So, you gentlemen have the rest of the week to make your decision."

Tom straightened in his seat. "Don't need the rest of the week. I'm with you."

Earl looked at me, his gray eyes entangled in tormented wrinkles. "Me too."

22

"You mean your dad went through the same mess?"

Audrey stopped in her tracks between the kitchen table and the sink and stared at me hard. She held two plates with the remnants of another late dinner, and I could see a slight tremor in her hands.

My eyes dropped to the silverware still on the table. "That's what Eddy said."

"And your dad never told you anything about it?"

"Well, he said things I didn't understand at the time. 'Those guys'll never get me back on the board, not the way *they* run things.' He repeated that a lot.

"After we made Dave a signer, he said, 'You don't understand the battles I've fought over this, Jim.' I thought at the time, 'But I do understand! I witnessed every single one of them.' But apparently I hadn't. I only witnessed the aftermath."

Audrey turned and went to the sink. "Now I understand why your dad blew up at meetings."

"No kidding. He never saw Schneider's adultery or embez-zlement resolved. But he didn't say a word about them, either."

"Pretty big secrets to carry."

"And carry alone." I looked up. "But he didn't turn a blind eye. Eddy says that Dad told Schneider to his face he should leave the ministry."

Audrey raised her eyebrows. "That was your dad. Makes me kind of proud of him."

I nodded and smiled for the first time in days. "Yeah. He was tough. No pressure ever kept him from speaking his mind."

Audrey's face went dark again and she sat down. "I just wish we'd known. We spent all those years being embarrassed by him—being angry. We could've shown him some sympathy. 'Dad, we understand. You did the right thing.' Maybe we could've given him some peace."

I went back to polishing the silverware with my eyes. "Yeah. But he was angry over lots of things."

"He was. But I still wish we'd known."

"He was angry over stuff I did, stuff Mom did. The church was just one area."

"I know that. But if we had known, we could've understood him better."

"We could've understood the church stuff, yeah. But not everything else."

Audrey found my eyes, but her look was indecipherable. "Jim, maybe the rest of his anger wouldn't have mattered so much to us. I don't know. If we could've helped him calm down about the church, he might've calmed down about other things, too. That's all I'm saying. Maybe we could've helped if we'd known."

I refocused on my greasy knife. "Did he strike you as the sort of man who liked help?"

Her voice hardened. "I don't mean counseling, Jim. Just understanding."

"We wouldn't have helped. We would've been angry right along with him—at least I would have. Anyway, he's gone now."

Audrey sighed and took our glasses to the sink. I could hear the faucet running and Audrey's quick swipes at the dishes. She picked them up with a crack and slapped them down again. She smacked the faucet off and sat down again.

We didn't say anything or look at each other. At length she stirred in her seat. "It's so horrible."

"What, Dad's battles?"

"No. What he was fighting is horrible. It's horrible that he lost."

"Yeah."

"I can't believe our church has been so corrupt."

I glanced up briefly and then heard my Professional Jim voice. "Well, the guys only did what they thought was right."

She looked at the ceiling and then at me. Her eyes were blazing. "Why do you men do that?"

"Do what?"

"Stick up for other men when you know they're wrong. You hate what the board did back then—every bit as much as I do—but you correct me as if it's so much more complicated than I could possibly understand. It's not more complicated. Those old men failed the church. They as good as lied by covering it all up. They let Pastor Schneider off so easy, it's sickening. They didn't do anything for the woman he was carrying on with—just ushered her away. And, maybe worst of all, they made a fool of Mrs. Schneider, the most dignified lady I can remember."

"I'm sorry."

"They pretended everything was fine, and this church has gone in circles ever since. Really, this mess with Dave is the board's fault, because they didn't learn their lesson the first time. I won't listen to anything in their defense."

"I'm sorry."

"'They're *the guys*. They don't mean any harm!' It's like men have no core."

I winced. "I patronized you. I'm sorry."

The Audrey I knew—the wife I had driven away with my anger early that morning—came back into her eyes, as if rushing to a window, bracing her hands on the pane, and searching.

"You're right. I'm pretending it's more complicated when it isn't. What the board did was horrible and I insulted you by suggesting otherwise." I sighed. "Plus, I didn't listen to what you were saying about Dad."

She was silent.

"You just wish we'd known what Dad went through. I wish that, too, and I'm sorry I cut you off instead of just agreeing."

Audrey's shoulders remained taut, but her eyes softened.

"Learning what Dad went through has helped me make peace with him—somewhat. I need to go further, and I think that's what you were telling me."

Silence.

"I'm very prideful, Audrey. I see that now. Too prideful to admit how angry I am at Dad, or at the board—or even at Dave." I shrugged and shook my head.

Audrey continued to stare, as if looking at something over my shoulder.

"Everybody says men aren't relational, aren't sensitive to emotions. Truth is, men are too relational. They're swayed by what others think just as much as women—if not more. They're prideful."

Audrey raised her eyebrows. "And women aren't?"

"Well, women are more forthright than men. When a woman's offended, she gives the offender the cold shoulder, maybe snipes a little. She wants the other party to know she's ticked off. Most men can't stand the thought of that. It hurts their vanity. They have to show how big they are. Men will only confront something when their anger reaches a fever pitch. And then they pretend like it never happened, just to prove they're tough. Just like the old westerns: the guys may come to blows, but they take any excuse, like somebody falling in the horse trough, to start laughing again. Anything not to look petty."

"Is that what went wrong with the church? Prideful men?"

"Maybe. Schneider was one of the guys—that much I remember. He had a camaraderie with the other guys, so they didn't want to blame him—not even for adultery and theft. Just like the guys didn't want to blame Dave tonight. Just like I didn't want to blame the guys a minute ago. There is something hollow in men. In me."

Audrey's face went dark again. "I don't get it."

"I'm hollow."

She shook her head. "You're doing the right thing, Jim, standing up to the board. I'm proud of that."

"It's just Dad, chapter two."

Audrey remained pensive, saying nothing for what seemed like forever. When she spoke, her voice was a hoarse monotone. "You're so much more effective than your dad, Jim. You have a way with words like no one I've ever known—like he certainly never had. You have more self-control, too. And I know you'll do what's right, not just what you think is right. You search for the right thing and you don't rest until you find it." Her voice dropped to a whisper. "And you're the only man I know who's able to change. You're not hollow, Jim."

I held my face in my hands and massaged my eyes. "I don't know who I am anymore."

"Jim, you're exhausted."

"No, it's more than that."

We were silent again and I couldn't move. I heard Audrey's blouse whisper as she leaned toward me, her voice a little nearer. "You've never talked this way before."

"I've never felt this way before."

"I know something's happening to you. But I can't see what it is."

I lifted my face from my hands.

She was staring at me with a quizzical look. "It's like—"

"What?"

"No, it's too weird."

"Please, Audrey. Say it anyway."

"It's like God is shaping you."

"Why is that weird?"

"I don't know. I guess we never talk about God as if he's actually alive."

My lips pulled to one side. "No, we don't. We're practical people, but now nothing works. And he's abandoned me."

"How can you say that?"

"He's gone. The way I used to think about God is worthless now."

"Why do you say he's abandoned you?"

"God won't put up with the way I treat people. He hates my hypocrisy."

The lines in her forehead shifted. "What do you mean, the way you treat people?"

I looked her in the eye. "I give grace when it suits me."

A touch of warmth came into Audrey's eyes.

"My grace isn't real. I use it to get better performance out of people, and then I withdraw it. God won't tolerate a fake."

"I don't think you're a fake, Jim. Even if you're inconsistent, God isn't going to throw you away."

"If he won't tolerate me, he has to throw me away. There's no practical difference between the two."

Audrey's fingers went to her temples and her eyes shut tight. "I don't know what to say to you. God knows how to restore us. We have to believe that." She leaned closer and scrutinized my face. "If you're a fake—and I'm not buying that for a minute, but if you are—God will show you how to change."

"But all I feel is guilt."

Her shoulders shot up. "I don't see why you should feel guilty when Dave's the liar. He's the fake, not you."

I stared at my crumpled napkin.

"Jim, why are you beating yourself up?"

I sat up in my chair. "I was wrong about Dave at every point. All my confidence was based in pride—and, therefore, sin."

"Oh, Jim, that's too much!"

"No, listen. Go back to the beginning. Dave volunteered that he'd ridden with Kim and then he played along while I counseled him. I only pierced that lie by a couple of accidents—asking 'by-the-way' questions that made him scramble. Columbo, without the brains. He volunteered more, all the stuff about Amy, and went along again while I played the part of wise, older counselor."

"You couldn't have known."

"My point is, I fell for his lies because I had all the answers. I was inflating my ego. Dave flattered me and almost got away with it. My confidence was sin."

Audrey sighed. "So you're beating yourself up because you were tricked."

"No. I was tricked because I was prideful. Being tricked just exposed me, started me asking questions."

"I see." Audrey's eyes went to the table and she leaned forward. "I see what you're saying. But I still think God is shaping you somehow. You need to trust him."

"How do you know he's shaping me?"

"I know because—no, it sounds too silly."

"What?"

Audrey sat back and pursed her lips. "Your voice has changed again."

How did she know about my voice? "What do you mean, *again*?"

"When we were first married, I was"—she looked away, elbows pulling in—"I was afraid. You could be so loud and I didn't understand. I thought you were always mad at me. But one day, years into our marriage, your voice changed. You were softer, almost hesitant. I'd always thought you didn't listen, but I realized you were listening—your way. God had done something in you that I didn't know about. So I figured I'd better stop judging you."

Her gaze returned to my face.

"You were right. I didn't know how to listen. Still don't."

Audrey reached across the corner of the table and put her hand on my forearm. "But you changed. I don't know what happened or how, but you were different. I love you for that change. I've never seen any other man do it."

"But what I became is"—I sighed again—"I'm still so self-serving."

"Yes, you are." She smiled and pressed my arm. "You're never going to be Superman, Jim. I know you hate the thought of being ordinary, but you'll have to live with it. If you see something wrong, then do what you do best: make the change."

The more she talked, the more my stomach tightened. Confessing my hypocrisy and pride was all well and good, and it probably satisfied her. But my skirting the issue of Flynn was itself a form of hypocrisy. Again I could see my mom wincing. How real was this conversation going to get?

The phone rang. I rose and took the call. After a brief exchange, I hung up and turned to Audrey. "There's no going back now. They got him. He was speeding down the interstate. Alone. Kim must've refused to go with him. Maybe their relationship wasn't as authentic as he thought."

"Or maybe he left her, too."

"Maybe." I recalled the look on Kim's face at the Bean. "She probably didn't know about the money."

Audrey sighed and brought her hand to her mouth. "What is Amy going to do? And the kids?"

I sank back into my chair and shook my head.

"How could Dave do this? Betray them?" Audrey's face had channels of tears.

I reached across the table and laid my hand on hers. She grasped my hand, propped her forehead on her other hand, and sobbed. I watched pain that refused appeasement, and I felt like a quivering staff about to split. In my mind's eye, Mom's wince had cooled into basalt. Did I still have the right to support my wife?

"I'm scared, Jim. What if the church really does eat you alive?"

"Don't worry about me. Amy's *already* been eaten alive."

"I know, I know. But I'm still scared. You're my husband, and anything that happens to you happens to me. I want you to be honored for telling the truth, but I'm afraid they're going to hate you. I don't see why you have to pay the price for Dave's sins. They should take it out on him."

I put my other hand on hers. "We don't know that's going to happen. They may rally when they hear the truth."

She wiped her face. "Are you afraid?"

"Yes." I looked away. "But not of them."

"What do you mean? Who else is there to be afraid of?"

I didn't answer.

A car door slammed outside, and we heard Rachel's voice saying good-bye to her friends. The front door opened and she whisked inside, her smile still glowing and her cheeks red. She slid her jacket off and tossed it on a hook. When she turned and saw us, she compressed her lips, staring at Audrey's tears. The pleasure left her eyes.

My face pulled tight and I heard Audrey's sniffles.

Rachel looked at the floor and then at me. "Is Pastor Dave fired?"

I stood and walked to her. She embraced me tightly, pressing her cheek into my chest. I enfolded her and she pressed tighter. She took a deep breath and sighed without a sound. I rested my hand on her head and stroked her hair, so soft it eluded my conscious touch but fascinated my fingers. It was as fine as when she was small. The moon seemed to pause over our silence, and I drank my innocent happiness as if it were unexpected water on my palate.

With Rachel still cleaving to me, I guided her to the table. "Let's talk, honey."

"It's all true, isn't it. He's fired."

I relaxed my arm from her shoulder but she wouldn't let go. "We have to talk about something else first, Rachel."

"What else is there to talk about? There can't be anything worse."

"Let's just talk. About you and me." I sat and she slid onto my lap like when she was five, her face remaining against my chest as if she were eavesdropping. Audrey and I stared at each other. Then she reached and massaged Rachel's neck. Again, the world seemed to pause around us, the knotted complexities of betrayal and deceit severed by my daughter's tender touch.

I finally spoke, though hardly making a sound. Rachel might only feel the rattle of my voice in my chest. "I've hurt you."

She tensed, her whole body on alert. "What do you mean?"

"Your windshield."

"It's okay, Daddy."

"No."

The tension remained.

"No, I don't think it's okay. I really hurt you."

She was still. "We don't have to talk about it."

"Yes, we do."

Audrey stared at me fixedly, her hand now moving up and down Rachel's back. Rachel was still leaning hard against my chest, and she didn't budge.

"Please tell me how I hurt you."

"You don't know?"

"I *think* I know. I could play it safe and not ask—or not listen to your answer. But playing it safe won't solve my problem. I need to change."

"I can't tell you what to change."

"Just tell me how I hurt you."

"I still don't want to talk about it."

"Please, honey."

After a long silence, she began haltingly, "I don't understand you, Daddy. You yelled at me and I had no idea what I even did. I didn't know what to fix. It's like you couldn't yell at anyone else, so you yelled at me. I still don't know how I broke it."

She didn't relax yet, but her voice grew stronger. "I said I was sorry and I meant it. But I don't even know what I was apologizing for. I guess I was irresponsible not to notice the crack. That's the only thing I know was wrong, because I really wasn't tailgating."

Her shoulder was still hard against my chest. "Sometimes I just give up trying to please you. I know it's wrong, but I can't help it. I can't do anything right."

I said nothing, but I felt her relax ever so slightly.

"I just want you to be nice, Daddy."

"Honey, I'm sorry."

The rigidity in her shoulders released and now she was cuddling.

"You're right: I yelled at you because I could get away with it. I'm sorry. I made you feel like you broke the windshield when you didn't break it. Those cracks happen to everybody. Making you apologize was cruel and pointless. Playing the generous father—'I'll pay for the windshield' (even though we know it was your fault)—was even worse. Will you forgive me?"

Her breath came and went, came and went, amid a silence that was now agonizing. "Why are you talking this way?"

My insides seemed to shrivel like dying weeds. There would be no moisture for me here. "Rachel, I have been dealing with a fake and a fraud for the past two days. I've learned more about deception than I ever wanted. And now I see the same deceit in myself—and I don't like it. I want to be real."

"You're not a fake, Daddy. Not like Pastor Dave."

"But I still need your forgiveness."

"I don't think you're a fake."

"Okay. But I've been mean to you and I need to change. That's why I'm talking this way."

"Daddy, you . . ."

I waited, but she was silent. "What is it, honey?"

She sighed and then finished in a burst. "You yell at me a lot. I've been scared of it since I was little. You're not going to change just because we had one little talk—no matter how much I want you to."

Audrey's head drooped and her hand paused on Rachel's back.

I swallowed and took a breath. "You're right. I hate the thought of it, but I'm going to be mean again sometime. It'll take me a while to learn how to be considerate. I'm so sorry."

Rachel relaxed completely in my arms. "I forgive you, Daddy."

"Please be patient with me."

"I love you. I'll keep loving you no matter what."

"I love you too."

Audrey's face shone like a dying saint's. She patted Rachel's shoulder. "You'd probably better get up now. Your father's circulation isn't what it used to be."

Rachel straightened and kissed me. "Thank you."

Audrey stepped slowly toward the stove, dragging her fingers along my shoulder as she went. She turned on the burner under the kettle, retrieved a box of tea, and set it on the table. Rachel moved to the chair next to mine and leaned against my shoulder. We sat in silence for a while, and I replayed the conversation with Rachel in my mind. Audrey cleared the glasses and silverware from the table and put the last few dishes into the dishwasher. Then she busied herself wiping down the counter.

When the kettle started to whistle on the stove, I dropped a tea bag into a mug and spoke to Rachel. "Back to your question: Yes, Pastor Dave is going to be fired."

"Good." Her voice had a note of finality.

"Well, there's more."

"More?"

"Dave stole a lot of money from the church. You were right. He could barely afford to take his family on trips, much less the other woman. So he used church money."

Tears gathered around her eyelashes. "Oh, Dad. What's going to happen?"

"He's going to jail."

She stared up at me, uncomprehending. "What's going to happen to Amy? What about Derek and Amanda?"

"I don't know, honey. We'll have to help them somehow. We're not going to abandon them."

"But they're going to see their daddy go to jail. How can anybody help them with that?"

"Honey, I know it sounds trite, but we're going to have to trust God. No one knows how to turn this around—I certainly don't."

Audrey came back to the table with the hot water. "I think we'll all have to change. Life will be different at church, no matter what. We may as well get it right this time."

"Exactly." I tugged at my tea bag as it steeped. "God will help us do that. He's not going to throw us away."

The phone rang again. Audrey went to answer, and her face brightened. "Oh, hi, Erin."

I felt a familiar knot beginning to form in my gut, and I thought, *Lord, your timing is impeccable.*

Audrey was silent for some time; her forehead crinkled as she listened. Then she looked at me with her amused expression. "Sweatpants, huh?"

"This about Dad?" Rachel's eyes had come alive.

Audrey nodded and spoke back into the phone. "Yeah, he's freaking us all out today."

Rachel leaned toward Audrey. "Please tell me she got a picture!"

Audrey listened more and then turned her head to Rachel. "It's hanging in the break room. Melissa's phone camera."

Rachel's smile was triumphant.

Audrey gazed at me. "Oh, that's sweet, Erin. He's just fine."

Audrey hung up and sat down next to Rachel. "All joking aside, Erin was very concerned about you, Jim. All your girls care about you over there. She wanted to be sure you got home safe."

"They're not 'my girls' anymore. You're my only girls."

Audrey and Rachel looked at each other, and Audrey's hand reached for mine. "We can share you."

"Fine, but I'm not going to share myself."

"What do you mean?"

"I don't know what Flynn just told you, but I was way too free talking to her this morning. Way too free. I realized after I left the bank that I had stepped over the line—at least in my own heart. I need to confide in *you*, Audrey, not in her."

I looked at my wife's face, every line soft with vitality. "I'm sorry for breaking that confidence."

Audrey didn't hesitate. "I forgive you, Jim. And I trust you."

I closed my eyes and drew my girls into a warm embrace.